PRIDE

P A WILSON

Ebook ISBN: 978-1-990509-16-2
Paperback ISBN: 978-1-990509-17-9
Audio book ISBN:978-1-990509-18-6

FREE EBOOK

Claim your copy of Buying Into Death when you use the QR code to sign up for my newsletter and follow Charity as she solves her fastest case yet!

1

I grabbed the coffee David handed me like it would save my life. After two months, I was still waiting for him to become tired of my nonsense and leave. Instead, he was half moved in, was friends with my friends, and fed me breakfast. Why couldn't I trust he'd keep doing it? Or that I wouldn't do something to make him run?

"Are you ready to talk yet, Charity?" he asked.

I hoped he'd just forget the conversation. Granted, he had a point about me going behind his back to meet a source on my last case. But nothing happened. The guy was an accountant; what was he going to do? Audit me to death? Okay, I didn't relish the idea of any kind of audit, but it wouldn't put me in the hospital, either.

"Aren't you on your way to work?" If I delayed enough maybe he'd forget about it. "I mean we can't stop in the middle so you can run off to keep our streets safe from criminals."

He picked up his phone and showed me the text he'd sent to his boss. *Running late.*

"Fine, how about I say sorry, and we just move on?"

We'd been down this path before, and nothing changed. He wanted me safe; I needed to take risks to do my job. Just because I wasn't a cop with a gun and a badge like him didn't mean I couldn't work my cases.

"We keep getting stuck." He topped up his coffee. "You think I'm trying to get in your way. I'm not. You do what you want and then say sorry. Then you do it all again."

I couldn't look him in the eyes, and the only other view was the finger dock outside my front door. Even I couldn't pretend to be fascinated by the concrete and floats for more than a few seconds. I didn't deliberately go out of my way to annoy him. I needed to be free to act on tips and to do my job.

"So, what do you want to do? If you can't deal with me as I am, you don't have to be here." Why did I say stuff like that? I'm not a kid. And I didn't want him to go. I might love him... but saying the words was a step too far.

"I'm not going anywhere," he said. "Unless you're done with me, I'm here for good."

I didn't say anything. What could I say?

"I took risks before," I said. If we were going to have this conversation, I could try to be honest about my feelings. "It feels like you don't believe I can do my job."

"I'm not trying to stop you," David said. He reached out and touched my hand. "When you disappear, I'm afraid you aren't simply following a clue, but that someone has beaten you, again."

It hadn't been that often. Although, his definition of too often probably differs from mine. "I'm not eager to end up in the hospital again either. I am careful." Ugh, now I sounded whiney. If this is what love does to me, I'm out. "Most of my cases are administrative stuff. I don't run after murderers every time. I don't expect you to call me every time you go out to catch a criminal."

He raised an eyebrow. I wasn't going to let him off the hook with that. If he had a real reason for the difference between us, he needed to say so. I wasn't a regular civilian. I was a successful private investigator.

"I'm part of a team," he said. "If I go missing, someone will come looking. If you go missing, no one knows. I don't want to read your name on a list in the morgue."

"Drama Queen. The last time my life was in danger you were right there. In fact, I was only involved because the cops needed my help."

"Yes, but you didn't do as we asked. You went in after her, you pushed until she started to fight." He emptied his mug and shoved it to the center of the table. "We're off topic. I'm aware you have to follow the case. I don't want you to stop being you. I want to know when I need to send in the cavalry."

It doesn't feel like that. "You help me with information, why isn't that enough?" My head didn't want to fight on this but every instinct kept me from agreeing. I wouldn't promise anything I couldn't guarantee.

"Think of this as more assistance. I swear I won't try to stop you. I think you are very capable. You've solved some pretty dangerous cases."

"So, what do you want? This argument needs to end. It's going to get in the way all the time."

He leaned back in his chair like I'd said something profound that he had to think over. Hadn't I asked him this before? Or had the words only happened in my head?

"If you got into trouble, or thought you might be getting into trouble, would you call Val? Or Matthieu? Or any friend?" He asked.

Light started to dawn. "I've done it before." *Let him say it.*

"But not me? You don't ask me for advice, and I've heard you ask Rory about a client."

"Because you are a cop." I shook my head when he tried to speak. "You have to uphold the law. How can I ask you for advice on nosing around if what I'm doing might be a little shady? How can I ask you about a source when they might be a criminal?"

"I thought this was all about controlling you," he said. "So, you are protecting me? You don't need to do that."

I wasn't going to tell him he also tried to protect me way too much. Maybe because it was all in my head. "How do I know where the lines are?"

"We can figure the details out," he said. "As long as you don't ask me to look away while you kill someone, we should be fine. Keep the details vague. I promise I won't bring you into protective custody for taking a risk."

"I can try that." I didn't have a case even close to risky right now, so it was an easy thing to say.

My phone rang before he could do anything more than nod.

2

I looked at the caller ID, expecting it to be unknown. So many spam calls came in at this time in the morning that I started ignoring them ages ago. If I didn't need to be available for clients, I'd turn the phone off until noon.

Blackhouse? So, someone in my contacts. I couldn't remember anyone with that name, but I'd developed the habit of entering everyone I encountered in the list. You never knew when a casual contact could end up as a client. Or a source.

I accepted the call but didn't say anything.

"Ms. Deacon?" A woman's voice.

"Speaking."

"Oh. I'm not sure if you remember me." She paused like she was sure I'd seen her name and hoped I would tell her where we met.

I recognized the voice, but still couldn't come up with the connection.

"We talked when your friend went missing," she said.

"You had a child with a temper." Glenda, that was the

name. And she'd lied about seeing Val. I almost ended the call.

"Oh, yes. Nora has calmed down a lot over the last year. I wonder if you would meet me for coffee? I might need to hire you."

I could use a new case. My active ones were all winding down and I got antsy when I had free time. I couldn't let go of the thought that if she hadn't lied, Val might not have endured a beating. I prefer to work with people I can trust. Or I work with clients who haven't yet given me a reason to distrust them. The last time I ignored that rule, I'd almost been killed.

"My schedule is quite full," I said. David gave me a questioning look. He knew I was free. I waved at him to wait. "When did you want to meet?"

She hesitated long enough that I thought about hanging up. "Can you come to my home, after lunch? Say one-thirty?"

"Can I call you back on this number?" I wanted to do a little research before I agreed. Or at least test out David's commitment to helping rather than interfering. "I need to check my availability."

Another pause. Everything she'd said or done up to this point made my gut yell at me to say no.

"Yes. This number is fine. I hope you can be free."

I ended the call.

"Since when are you overloaded with cases?" David asked. He was pulling on his jacket, ready to head to work.

"I'm not sure I should go," I said. "I met her during an old case. Before we met. She lied and it was about something important. And she said she might need to hire me but not why and then didn't call."

"Is it likely to be dangerous?" He didn't look at me when he asked.

I considered. Yes, she bent the truth, but Val survived, and I remember thinking there must be a problem when I talked to her the first time. That kid was in full-on tantrum, and we only exchanged a few words. "I don't think so. I don't like the idea of working with someone who started the relationship with a lie. It left Val in a bad position. But she's likely looking for background checks or maybe proof of whether her husband is cheating or not."

"It can't be the first time a client lied to you," he said. "Do you want my advice?"

He was trying. Time for me to meet him halfway and not assume he wanted to keep me from doing my job because it might be risky. "Yeah."

He sat and reached for my hand. "Do you know why she lied?"

"About seeing Val? No. You think she had a good reason? Someone beat Val half to death while we ran around searching for her."

"People lie all the time," he said. "You know that. If she'd told the truth, would it have made any difference? Would you have found Val sooner?"

No. But it didn't make it okay for her to lie. "Maybe. I have no idea what she was hiding. I doubt it's the same thing after this much time."

He squeezed my hand. "You should meet her. You can turn down the job, but you might find out why she didn't remember seeing Val. And maybe she needs your help more than you need to find out the truth."

Who was this guy? It kind of bothered me he knew me so well. It also bugged me that he sounded reasonable, and I sounded petulant. The incident with Val was in the past. She was alive and happy with Rory, and her business was thriving. If Glenda had told me the truth, maybe none of the good things would have come to Val either. "I would like to hear why she thought I could help that long ago." I reached for the phone.

"Just be careful," David said.

"I am always careful." He laughed at me, which made me smile. "Okay, I'm mostly careful."

"And your instincts are solid," he said. "Leigh told me about a lot of your previous cases when we first met. If you think there's something wrong, there probably is."

That didn't mean I'd refuse the job. Sometimes a little something not quite right is interesting. "I might need you to do a bit of research."

"You want me to check if she's got a record?"

"I can do that." I had access to most of the official records through various channels, authorized and not totally legal. "I'll let you know."

"Whatever you need." He kissed me. "I'll try not to get fired for helping you."

Was this the way it should work? A cop and a private investigator giving each other some support? We'd see when things got sticky in an investigation. He was right; my instincts were good. I just didn't always pay attention in the way I should.

I called Mrs. Blackhouse back and confirmed our appointment. Then I printed out a blank engagement form. If I agreed to take the case, I needed her signature. And a substantial upfront payment.

I spent the next hour researching her.

She didn't post much on social media, so nothing to

support my gut feelings. I didn't know what I expected. People who committed crimes were like everyone else online — only posting things that made them look good. But my feelings didn't go away.

3

The street looked exactly the same as I remembered. Mature neighborhoods with houses protected by Heritage status, making them safe from redevelopment. Also, the lack of profit from pulling down a couple of multi-million-dollar single family homes to fight for permission to build condos at a low density and not turn enough profit might be a good reason.

The sidewalks were bumpy from tree roots. The same trees provided shade and a slippery carpet of leaves. When I arrived at the Blackhouse address, I took a moment to check it out. The yard was finished unlike the last time; it was neat, contained landscaping that needed a professional to keep up. The entrance was up a flight of steps to a wide porch and a bright blue door. There was another door on the ground floor, tucked in beside the stairs. Most of these designed for rentals, legal or not, to help with the mortgage. Here, clearly not a living space. No path, no welcome light above the door.

I didn't see any other access points. Or exits, which were what I'd been hoping to identify. Despite my assurances to

David that this was going to be easy, I still had an uneasy feeling in my gut.

The gate opened smoothly, no creak on the stairs to give Mrs. B warning. I knocked, and she answered immediately. Either she'd been looking out or there was a security system hidden in the azaleas.

"Come in. I have coffee ready." She looked less frazzled than that last time. Dark hair pulled back into a ponytail, makeup perfect, dark skirt and perfect cashmere sweater.

"It shouldn't take long," I said. "I need a few details about the case so I can figure out where to slot it in my calendar."

"I hoped you could start today," she said, leading me through a hall to the kitchen at the back of the house.

The decor inside the house was clean and modern. Outside, if you ignored the cars, it could be a century ago. In here, white and grey cabinets lined the walls. High-end appliances gleamed in their built-in nooks. An espresso machine lurked on the counter, and black stools stood in a row on the far side of an island. Apparently, heritage restrictions only applied outside.

Nora sat at a child's table drawing.

"Is the issue urgent?" I asked. My plan to pretend I couldn't take the case for a month or two so I wouldn't need to say no, was already sidelined. I'm not good at that kind of thing. Spinning a lie in the moment, not a problem. Lying long term became too complicated and difficult pretty fast. And I tried to make sure I only really lied to bad guys.

"I think it might be," she said.

"Tell me what you need, and we'll see," I said. "Is there a problem with your daughter?"

"Nora?" she looked confused.

"When I met you earlier, you had some concerns. I thought it was about the adoption."

She pulled coffee cups out and placed them on the counter. "She did have some trouble adjusting. But no, not Nora. Espresso?"

"Mrs. Blackhouse, I am busy, can we get down to business?"

"Call me Glenda," she said. "Of course, you have other clients. I just... well it's taken me a while to get to the point of reaching out."

Her hesitancy didn't help me figure out what to do. I'd had the odd reluctant client before. Spouses who suspected infidelity but weren't sure they wanted proof. I hated to be the one to confirm their suspicions, and in all but one case, the suspicions were correct.

"You did call, though," I said. "I can go if you've changed your mind. But whatever you are worried about won't go away with me."

Nora came over and tugged on Glenda's skirt.

"Mama, look." She held a crumpled drawing and shoved it at her mother.

"It's beautiful," she said. "Who is this?"

Nora pointed at me and then hid behind Glenda, her eyes huge.

I looked over. Stick figures, a little one holding the hand of a slightly bigger one. A large dad figure loomed behind. Glenda pointed to a person on the edge of the picture. Stick Charity, although I wouldn't have known without the kid pointing at me.

"Go draw some more." Glenda gave Nora a pat and a gentle push toward the table.

The kid dutifully ran back to her art.

Glenda put the picture on the counter, smoothing it out.

"I don't want her hurt. I might not do anything with the information you find. It took so long for us to find a child to adopt. My husband was reluctant at first to take her. He worried we'd run into cultural challenges since she came from India. But no one seemed to care."

"That's up to you. But you haven't told me anything." I wasn't going to ask the obvious question. She had to be the one to say the words because she was going to have to live with the consequences. Even if she did nothing with the results, the knowledge couldn't be put aside.

"My husband is acting oddly," she blurted out. "It started about a month ago. I don't know if he's having an affair or if it's something else."

At least now we could move forward. An easy case. Figure out what hubby was up to and done. A few days' work. No danger, so David would be happy.

I pulled the agreement out of my purse. "I can start later today if you are ready."

She didn't hesitate. I guess now that she'd stated the big fear, everything else seemed like just details. She signed the document, took it to another room to copy, wrote the check and handed both over.

"Does your husband have access to this account?"

"He doesn't have a clue it exists," she said, then gave a bitter laugh. "My mother divorced twice. She told me to always have my own money. I hated the idea of hiding something from Alan, but I did as she advised. Now I realize that love haze at the beginning of a marriage fades away. You find out you married a human being. I've set up an account for Nora, so she can be independent. Maybe she'll make better choices."

I put the check in my pocket and started pulling the details out of Glenda.

4

I finished ordering dinner and got back to my paperwork. I tended to my other cases before starting on Glenda's. One case was on hold until the client got back to me, so I had time and a need for cash flow. The Blackhouse job filled the hole. Sending reports and invoices let my brain mull over the meeting.

"I'm home," David said as he came through the door. The one time he'd just walked in, I almost beaned him. Now he announced his presence.

"Dinner's twenty minutes out," I said. "I'll be done by then."

He came around to give me a kiss and I didn't close my laptop in time to hide my notes.

"Blackhouse? That's your new client?"

"Yes. Usual marital stuff." I turned the laptop away because I couldn't shut it now he'd seen the information. "I ordered Thai food."

"Sounds good." He tossed his jacket on the back of a chair. "Did you ask her about Val?"

"Not yet." It hadn't seemed appropriate at the time, and I figured I would save the question for the end of the case. Or maybe as ammunition if I had to shock her out of something — like blaming the messenger. "How was your day?"

"Half the day in court. I got some paperwork done while I waited to be called. Got a lead on that murder."

If I could get him talking about his investigation, he'd leave me alone. I didn't have much to talk about, and I didn't want to listen to his advice. "The one in Burnaby? Shot in the head?"

He went to the fridge and took out two beers. I shook my head when he offered me one, so he put the second bottle back. "Yeah. It could be gang related. Looked like a professional job. We didn't find anything linking the victim to anyone of interest — yet."

"Until today?" A gang murder could be hard to solve. Sure, most of them were clear cut. Someone gets caught ripping off the wrong guy, or sleeping with the wrong woman, or snitching. But gangs always had people on the outside who looked legit. The money launderers, the doctors who patched them up no questions asked. In those cases, finding the gang was harder, sometimes impossible.

"Yeah. Got a call from Andy Miller over at the RCMP. The victim was caught on a phone tap with Ivan Kuznetsov. Couple of months back. A coded conversation. Apparently, texts didn't catch on with Ivan's group. Anyway, now that we know which gang, it's only a matter of time."

Interesting. I don't have a contact in the Mounties. Maybe I could piggyback on David's. Or maybe not. I don't play well with authority. "I thought you hated the feds."

"Only when they get in the way." David finished off his beer. "I love them when they help."

I filed away the name, Andy Miller, and pulled my laptop over. "I need to do this before dinner so I can begin the investigation tomorrow."

He moved away and put his empty bottle in the recycle bin. "I need a shower. It's nice out; we should eat on the roof."

I nodded and started typing. Making notes about my impressions. Bullet points for everything that happened in the short time I met with Glenda. And some key steps that I would take tomorrow. I still hated this part of the case. I wanted to start digging into Alan Blackhouse, but over the years, I'd learned a few lessons about headlong rushes and wasted time. Getting this down now meant I didn't have to try to dig the details up from memory when I needed them. A couple of times, memory had been different from fact.

When I was done, I shut down and promised myself to enjoy the evening.

The security door buzzer caught my attention. I let the delivery guy in. I heard the shower stop right after. Perfect timing.

David joined me as I put the cartons on the table on my rooftop patio. Glasses and a chilled bottle of pinot grigio sat ready. The cutlery and napkins under a paperweight to keep the wind from stealing them.

It was a beautiful evening. The sun still warm, the breeze cool. The scent of the saltwater, and sound of the shore-birds. If you filtered out the traffic noise, and the tang of diesel, you could pretend you were on the beach at some idyllic resort.

"You forgot bowls," Dave said.

"I don't want to wash them," I said. "We can eat out of the cartons, like a picnic."

He settled in the chair opposite me and started opening

the food. "Sometimes I love your laziness-driven efficiencies."

"It doesn't mean you can cherry pick all the best stuff." I grabbed the Pad Thai and dug in.

"Do you want me to run a check on this Blackhouse?" He asked the question very casually, focusing on digging out shrimp from the curry.

"I prefer to do it myself." I did the same not looking at him thing. It felt weird that we were tiptoeing around the issue, but I didn't want an argument up here where the neighbors could hear. And I wanted to keep the favors I asked of him to a minimum. "Then I know I've completed the whole search."

"Okay. Let me know when I can help." He poured wine into both glasses.

"I will," I said. Then I couldn't hold back anymore. "We don't have to be super polite, David. I promise not to bite your head off for offering."

He grinned and my knees went weak. I'd never felt that before. Happy I'd made him happy. The weird thing for me was that I didn't even care that it was girlie. I just liked to make him smile.

"Don't make promises you can't keep," he said.

I pointed a chopstick at him. "Have faith, buddy."

"Seriously, don't wait until you are in trouble before asking for help, okay?" He picked up another carton. "You can be stubborn."

I had no reasonable argument to counter him. I left it too late in two cases with my other cop friend. Leigh had managed to dig me out of the hole, but I'd almost died before she arrived.

"If you promise not to foist help on me," I said, "then I promise to ask."

"Foist?"

I snorted curry laughing. When I got my breath back, I decided to take the favor. "If you can find out anything about Alan or Glenda Blackhouse without calling attention, that would be great."

5

W hen David left the next morning, I started the search for dirt on Alan Blackhouse. I needed something to follow. I'd meet him if I couldn't find anything, but that was always risky. I only had a few solid cover identities, and I didn't want to burn any if I could avoid it. I wanted enough detail on him to create a short toss-away story to make me appear legitimate in some way other than as a PI investigating him.

I found Alan listed as an Investment Advisor on LinkedIn, but no contact information. Odd, but not evidence of wrongdoing. People had empty profiles all the time. Maybe his business came from referrals, or he worked in-house for a bigger firm.

I didn't find him on the usual platforms, and Glenda's Facebook didn't show him in any pictures. Now my investigative senses were itching. Whatever he was up to, it wasn't normal for people to be fully offline when they had a business to run.

A search of local organizations had him listed so I had hope for other media; address and email but nothing else. I saved the contact information in my phone. The address was downtown, so unless he was pretending a PO Box was a unit number, he must have an office.

I set up alerts and did a bit more searching.

AFTER A COUPLE OF HOURS, I gave up. Alan Blackhouse was practically invisible online.

Time to take a different tack. Assuming the Financial Adviser information held some truth, what nefarious activities could he be involved in?

Money laundering? Embezzling? Ponzi scheme? When a lot of money floated around, it opened up infinite opportunities and temptations for crime.

I hated being stuck like this. When I first started my agency, I thought it would be all action. I got beaten up enough to realize a bit of knowledge before acting was smart. But it didn't help me when my impatience boiled up. And digging into electronic records was a sure path from crime stats down the rabbit holes of TikTok videos and cute baby goats.

I grabbed a jacket and left for a walk hoping to get my brain going again.

I HEADED FOR STANLEY PARK, picking up a coffee on the way. I didn't have time to do the whole seawall, I rarely had the time, and I never actually wanted that much exercise. I did have time to stroll around the lagoon and veer off to English Bay. That should be enough. And popcorn vendors lined the sidewalks at that destination.

I missed my partner, but Matthieu and Lu were still in France. And Lu was carrying a surprise baby, so they wouldn't be coming back until the child was old enough to fly. I needed to get used to being a lone operator again.

Was David right about me needing help? I figured he'd have a better idea of the kind of things Alan might be into, but his career would be in danger if he didn't take over a criminal case from what his bosses still considered a pain-in-the-ass amateur.

And maybe it was just an affair after all.

Maybe I should find out where Mr. Blackhouse hung out and just follow him around.

The view opened up as I neared the street. In fact, the park came to an abrupt end at a busy road. I decided to hang out at Second Beach for a bit, rather than committing to the hike that would take me to English Bay. As much as I wanted the fresh air, I needed to get the investigation going.

I dropped my coffee cup into a recycle bin and found a log in the sand to sit on. The sun glinted off the choppy water. A few kids were screaming in excitement over some incomprehensible game while moms chatted in the shade. A perfect afternoon if I wanted to waste time.

But I couldn't.

The realization that Alan might not be a criminal, as disappointing as it was, opened up a few more questions. Who? Man, woman? Both? Could it be a long history of infidelity? And his change of behavior might also just be something to do with his business.

And if he was a criminal, that list became more federal than local crime in a blink. The RCMP would be involved. I didn't enjoy keeping secrets from David about what illegal activities I found in my investigations — or any of the local cops for that matter. The mounties? A whole different scenario. I had no history with them, so no leverage. I really had no reason to think they would cause me problems. But if they did, I'm not sure I would extricate myself easily.

One of the kids sped past laughing and hiccupping as she outran her buddy.

Time to get back to work. I'd pick up my car and go find Alan's office if I couldn't find another clue online in the next hour.

BY THE TIME I got back, it was too late to make lunch, and I couldn't ignore the rumbling in my stomach. I grabbed the Thai leftovers and set them to nuke.

"Okay, Charity. No more excuses. You need to start earning your fee."

Since I'd ignored the chance that it was an affair, I started with the dating apps. A few were dedicated to cheating. I also put an alert on his credit card and bank, with a silent thanks to Glenda for handing over the codes.

I got a profile for Alan on one of the apps. But it was old and there didn't seem to be any activity.

The microwave pinged and I grabbed my lunch.

Having the codes for his credit card and banking was far better than using my semi-legal access to databases. I got to look at his spending history.

The transactions told me more than any of the searches I'd done in the past. "Thank you, Mr. Blackhouse."

He frequented a few clubs. I made notes of the names to confirm later, but some had been in the news lately. A bit of gang violence. It might not mean anything, but I had a contact who would help with that.

He also carelessly transferred funds to an account Glenda didn't know about. And he took the money from his business. Equipped with those numbers, I could go deeper.

I finished lunch, then set a trace request on his phone to make sure I had a chance to find Alan when I needed to. Knowing how to do a little hacking was key to a successful private investigation.

Time to head for East Van and my contact in the criminal underworld of Vancouver.

G uy was my contact in the Hells Angels. We had a mutual arrangement. He did me favors; I kept an eye on his nephew to stop him from joining a gang. To be honest I had the easiest part of the deal. The kid showed no interest in gang life, so I just checked in a couple of times a month. Guy said he worried about how easy it was to fall into a gang's activities. I figured the risk of Guy's own involvement in that world dragging the boy in kept him up most nights.

Today Guy wasn't answering my texts. He probably meant I should leave him alone, but I needed a way to get ahead on the case and that required persistence. If Alan was involved in something shady, and those clubs I found didn't cater to the casual trade, then Guy would know. And I'd find a way to make him tell me.

He might be able to avoid my texts, but I had a good idea where he might be in the afternoon; the Downtown Eastside hassling someone over a debt, or a drug shipment, or something else I didn't want to know about. So, I drove over and parked a few blocks away from Hastings and Main. My car would be fine and so would I. The people who did business on the streets here didn't want added attention.

I CROSSED Hastings glancing around for Harleys, figuring Guy wouldn't be too far from his bike. My phone rang as I headed north. David.

I couldn't tell him where I was and definitely not what I was doing. Our truce over his help didn't need to be tested so quickly.

"Hi." I kept my voice light and hoped none of the noise on the street tipped him off.

"How's the case going?"

"Slow, but it's only day one." Was I supposed to ask why he called? If I did, could I sound innocent?

"I have some information on your client and her husband," he said. "Well, what I found isn't much. Your Alan Blackhouse has some suspicious activity on his credit cards. And his phone's been cloned or something."

They could track his phone live? That would help when I needed his location. And I wouldn't have to burn favors to find out. "What do you mean? I know what cloned means, but how can you be sure?"

"It shows up in two places at the same time," David said. "The locations are weird for a straying spouse case. Enough that I reached out to a contact in the RCMP."

"You involved them?" No way the mounties would stay out of the way if Alan or Glenda were committing federal crimes. I knew it was a mistake to let David help so soon. We hadn't set any ground rules.

"Don't panic," he lowered his voice. "I didn't mention you. I said I didn't want to bump into anything they had going on. We do it all the time."

Horns started blasting as a junkie shuffled across the street. I don't know why people think the noise will speed things up. It was more likely to make the guy yell back and stand in the way for longer.

"What did he say?" I moved farther away from the commotion. "And what happens if they are looking at him?"

"Where are you?" A shouting match between a store owner and another junkie prompted that question.

"Downtown. I'm following up on something."

I heard him sigh. I guess I should be grateful he was trying not to tell me to go home and wait for him to take care of me.

"I'm fine, David. I need to follow up on leads if I'm going to solve any cases."

"Is it dangerous?"

"Not particularly." He wouldn't believe me if I said no. It wasn't a lie. This area wasn't physically risky, but it played hell on your emotions to see so much misery and not be able to do anything about the injustice. "I'll be fine. I'll make dinner tonight."

"Are you cooking?" he asked. "I mean, is dinner takeout? Should it be takeout? Should I cook?"

"Very funny." I couldn't deny my skills were more on the ordering side of the equation. "I'll make a salad. You bring the wine."

"Maybe I'll have some answers for you by dinner," he said. "Be careful, okay?"

I felt the old familiar rush of defensiveness. I knew how to take care of myself. I managed for years before he came along. Yes, I ended up beaten and in the hospital more than once, but I was still alive and fully functioning. I pushed the annoyance away; he didn't mean I wasn't capable. He cared. "I will. See you later."

I texted Guy again immediately. No answer and not one Harley in sight. I stood on Cordoba wondering whether to turn toward the more commercial side of downtown or head east and hope the side streets would be more useful to me. I couldn't ask anyone if they'd seen the Angels without raising some suspicions.

A rumble sounded behind me. I pulled out my phone and pretended to be checking the GPS for directions. I held it up and turned slowly in a circle; no need to worry about this lost tourist.

Four Harleys cruised past me, attention on the road. They turned east on Cordoba and the last rider scowled at me. Guy.

If he thought a dirty look would stop me from following, he forgot who I was. Yes, the glare might be a warning, but I would be careful not to be caught by his buddies. I would track him down and take thirty seconds. Okay maybe a minute. The point is I'd be fast. Of course, I couldn't chase four motorcycles down the street for long. Fortunately, they turned and entered an alley a few blocks down. I decided to leave my car where I parked it and walk.

There was a slight risk they did notice me, so I took off my jacket and tied it around my waist. Now I looked like I belonged a bit more in my teeshirt and jeans. I pulled my hair out of the ponytail and messed it up a little as I walked toward the alley between a small grocery store and a tattoo studio. Time to pull on my slightly screwed up chick persona.

7

The alley smelled of damp earth, pee, and something rotting in the corner. I kept to the center of the gravel paving and listened for evidence of Guy's team. It did exit out to Hastings at the other end, so I had a second escape route. About halfway down, it split into a cross-alley. It's like whoever designed this area made it for illicit activities. I mean, why did you really need this many alleys?

At the intersection, I saw Guy standing guard. His buddies were doing something behind a dumpster; nothing violent, yet.

He didn't look my way, maybe on purpose. I didn't want to attract any other attention, but I wasn't going to leave here without talking to him.

I stood waiting for a few minutes, long enough to be sure Guy had seen me and purposely looked away. That, or he was a lousy lookout. I coughed, but he didn't react.

I pulled my keys out of my pocket and dropped them loudly. Then I swore.

Guy turned and glared at me. He cocked his head to

send me back toward the entrance. Then he turned and said something to his companions.

He moved toward me as I backed toward Cordoba.

"Far enough," he said.

We were in the shade of a lean-to beside the back door of the tattoo studio. He came at me faster than I expected and for a second, terror stuck me in place. Then I remembered it was Guy, not some random biker.

"Why haven't you been answering my texts?"

"Why don't you take the hint? I'm busy. And these guys won't take kindly to me talking to you."

Why did he think I'd taken the time to disguise myself? "They're occupied for a while, and this won't take long."

"Things are different now. If they figure out who you are, I'm dead."

Normally that would be figurative, but I had no illusions about it being literal. He'd never been worried about it before. "Why? I'm just a chick looking for a score."

"No. You are a cop's girlfriend."

Oh. I hadn't even thought about that being an issue. But I couldn't let him fob me off because of David. "He doesn't know what I'm doing. We'll be quick, and he won't even find out I'm here. What did you tell them?"

"I needed a piss."

"Okay, I need information about a guy named Alan Blackhouse."

"I said no."

He didn't walk away though. "Do they think you have prostate problems?"

"Maybe I decided to have a smoke, too."

"So, Alan Blackhouse?"

"Charity, this is too dangerous. Not just for me. Are you sure your boyfriend doesn't know about me?"

"He doesn't need to," I said. "So, we don't have an arrangement anymore?" He stared at me, and I realized what that might sound like to him. "Tony is fine now. I guess if you don't need me to help with him, you can walk away." No way I'd leverage the kid.

"I don't know anyone by that name."

We wouldn't have much more time. Whatever was going on behind the dumpster wouldn't take much longer. "I don't believe you. He hangs out in some of the same places you do."

"Lots of people do," he said. He looked back to the cross alley. "You got a picture?"

I dug around for my phone in my jacket pocket. I had one decent photo Glenda gave me. I found the email and waited for the image to load.

"What do you think he's doing?" Guy asked as the very slow Wi-Fi dealt with the file.

"I'm working for his wife." I turned the phone to him as soon as the photo appeared. "Him."

"Yeah. I see him around. And now you've crossed the line into way too dangerous. You need to drop the case. I mean it."

Why did every man in my life want to stop me from doing my job? It couldn't be my sex, or there would be other signs. Of course, the other side of the question was, why did I keep getting into situations that made men in my life tell me to drop it? "Did you see him at *Sila* two nights ago? I know you guys hang out there."

"We do some business with people in *Sila,*" he said. "For someone you don't want to meet."

"And Alan?"

He clearly wanted to walk away, but something kept him standing with me. "Same, I think."

He was staying because he knew I would just go to the club. I figured he was balancing the danger if I turned up there, and wondering if he'd told me enough to make me realize he was right. Well, he could keep hoping that. "What exactly does he do when he's there?"

Guy took a step closer. My back pressed against the fence. I had nowhere to go no matter how much I wanted to run. I clenched my fist and reminded myself this was Guy. He wouldn't hurt me. And if he wanted to? Well, I was a cop's girlfriend.

"He hangs out with someone who is working with a big shot. No clue what he does, maybe he's a wannabe, but this big shot? He does the kind of business we don't touch."

"What's the big shot's name?" If Alan was getting in with someone who scared Guy, maybe I should get Glenda away from him and not wait for proof.

"You don't need his name."

I could find out without him. If I kept digging, I would do it quietly. No reason Mr. Big Shot needed to find out anything about me. But if I didn't know who he was, I couldn't avoid him. "So, someone who deals in really ugly stuff. That narrows it down. People, right? I don't mean the regular hookers you guys run. Kids? Trafficked women?"

"Charity, what if I dropped a dime on you to your boyfriend?"

"And your boss might order you killed too," I said. "Russian?"

"They are complete assholes. They don't care everyone knows who they are. Like they can't be touched."

So, I'd hit it right. To be fair, there weren't that many options. "Okay. Thanks, I'll be careful."

"Be more than careful," he said. "Stay away."

"You can help by answering my texts, so I don't have to come looking for you."

A shout came from the direction of the dumpster. Guy's friends were looking for him.

"Get out of here," he said, then strolled back to the alley without looking back.

8

As soon as I dropped off the car and started walking home, it hit me how much of a risk I'd taken — chasing Hells Angels down an alley in an area of town where a woman's scream would result in turning the music up rather than a rescue attempt. Good thing I didn't think things through. Getting things done meant taking risks.

David would kill me if he found out. Then he'd go find Guy and make him pay for putting me in that situation. Not with violence, but Guy didn't live the kind of life that kept him off the cops' radar.

When I got to the security gate, I remembered about dinner. I needed to go buy the ingredients for a salad or grab a pre-made one and some extra protein to make it look like I'd done the assembly. But I didn't have the energy to go back to my car and head out grocery shopping. The only stores within walking distance came with premium prices and little choice unless something was organic and only handled by virgins on a full moon. My only option was to order something from my local restaurant.

I started shaking as soon as my door closed behind me. This was stupid. I'd done riskier things and never freaked out. I poured water into the coffee maker and pressed the power button. Yes, it was too late for caffeine, but these single serving ones made hot chocolate and tea as well. And I needed something comforting. And being inside my home didn't stop the shakes. So, that's why I needed hot chocolate, and four cookies.

When I stopped reacting, I called the restaurant and ordered dinner. I ran upstairs and showered off the smell of the alley. The delivery guy beat David to the door by two minutes, so I had no chance to pretend the food wasn't takeout.

"I thought we'd have a night in," David said. He placed a chilled bottle of pinot grigio on the counter and shrugged out of his jacket. "It's too cold to head up to the patio, and I have some info that you probably don't want the neighbors hearing."

"About Alan?" I opened the salad cartons and put the contents in bowls. Too many meals eaten from the takeout containers made me feel like I was well on my way to slobhood.

"Yeah. How was your day?" He grabbed cutlery and wine glasses.

"I got a few tips," I said. No details, or I'd be blabbing everything. "Follow up tomorrow. Unless your stuff is better."

"I heard back from the RCMP." He poured the wine and started digging into the seafood salad.

Was he drawing out the information because it was good? Or because it was nothing and he just wanted to milk the story?

"What did they say?" I wasn't planning on denying him

the pleasure of controlling how he wanted to share the story. Mostly because doing so kept me off the hook for the whole truth about my day.

"They don't have much in the way of real proof. You think your client might be okay with rumors?"

"I think she wants something she can use. Her gut is telling her something is wrong."

David nodded and continued eating. I picked through my greens for the good bits: scallops, salmon, shrimp.

"There's something," David said. "Andy didn't, or maybe couldn't, tell me much. Not unusual, we all keep things close until we amass enough to use."

"By then you wouldn't tell me because the information would be too sensitive." I tried for a laugh, but it didn't really work.

"Andy won't endanger a case for a favor," he said. "But maybe you can give him what you found."

Nice try. This was my case and I'd keep it that way. If this Andy guy couldn't give me anything, fair play. He had his job and I had mine. "Nothing much yet," I said. "Just some places he visits. People he might meet there. You know how it is this early."

He took our empty bowls and put them in the sink, then topped up my wine. "Andy wants you to back off."

"And what do you think?" The RCMP could actually kick me off a case, but not until I got in their way. I didn't plan on giving them that opportunity.

"The cop in me says you should leave this to the professionals."

"So what exactly did he say?"

"This is too dangerous. You might destroy a year-long investigation for a bit of marital strife."

"Everything is dangerous," I said. "Walking down the

street is dangerous in some places. And this isn't an argument taken too far. My client could be in danger, right? Or, am I reading this wrong?"

"What kind of places are you hanging out?"

I would not to let him push me into that fight. "What kind of investigation? If you want me to let my client go and wait for the professionals to deal with the danger, I need the details."

"I didn't say I wanted you to back off. I said the cop in me did. I know better than to tell you to stop. I prefer it if I'm not in the dark about what you're up to, but you'll go into stealth mode if you think I'm trying to butt in."

Still no details. But I got the feeling he guessed I wasn't at home doing Internet searches today. "What exactly did this guy say they had on Alan? Rumors work for me," I said.

"They think he's money laundering for one of the local gangs. A big one," David said. "I can guess. We are aware of the players."

I could guess too, but David would have more specifics than just the gang. "Who?"

"I'm not going to help you get involved." He wouldn't even look at me.

So, there it was. He promised to stop protecting me, but this was his loophole. "I'd be safer if I have all the information. Do you want me finding out by stumbling into a situation? I am not giving up."

"We need to end this right here." He picked up his jacket. "Charity, I agreed to let you do your job. Of course I did. And I know you are going to keep looking. But you can't ask me to send you off to be hurt."

"You're leaving?" How was I going to get him to spill if he left? That was better than the thought at the top of my mind. Was he going to come back?

"I'm going home. I'm too tired for an argument tonight. I'm not sure if I can avoid one if I stay."

He headed out and I didn't get a chance to say I would let it drop.

9

I didn't sleep well when I finally gave up the useless search and went to bed. Something I'd never felt before kept me too wound up to relax enough to drop off. When Jake was away from me, it didn't make any difference. I never thought he'd stay away. I never worried that I'd said something that would end our arrangement. Of course, I never saw the end coming either. With David, my gut twisted and burned at the thought we were through. And maybe the difference was that Jake and I only had an arrangement, one with fun and friendship, but not the big scary love word.

David hadn't called and I was too stupid to reach out. And he wasn't innocent in this. He'd brought the RCMP into my case. They would shut me down fast and put me in a cell if I kept investigating. Okay, maybe that was a bit of an exaggeration, but I couldn't let anyone sideline me. And so far, that was the only thing happening. I had nothing. It made me sure that there was something to find, because no one was that private no matter how hard they tried. Someone must have posted something about him somewhere.

Over breakfast an idea had filtered up through the fog and bitterness. I needed to talk to Alan Blackhouse.

I needed a cover story, and I needed to let my client know what I was going to do.

It was after nine, so Glenda should be alone in the house. If Alan was using the Investment Adviser cover, he would keep normal business hours.

I called, and Glenda confirmed she was alone.

"Your husband is pretty private," I said. I wasn't going to tell her the RCMP were looking at him. That would get me and David into all kinds of trouble. "I need to meet him."

"No. He'll want to know who you are and…"

"I have a cover story all worked out," I said. "He won't know I'm working for you."

She didn't speak when I paused. I heard Nora in the background singing some kids' song, high and repetitive.

"I promise he won't know. I wanted you to hear it from me. And if he tells you about this investigator, you need to act surprised."

"What's the story?"

"I'll tell him I'm looking into an adoption for a wealthy client, and I want his opinion of the agency you used." It should be good. I didn't need any new IDs. My own read Private Investigator. "Is there any reason I shouldn't ask?"

A long pause in which Nora switched songs.

"I don't think so, and he did everything with the agency, so it makes sense that you would talk to him."

"Good. If he asks, I'll say I found his name when I searched adoption records." Even if they were sealed, I would be able to rely on his probable assumption that a PI would be hacking records anyway. We do, don't get me wrong.

"Okay. Please, be very careful. He has a temper, and I don't want him to come home angry."

So there was some violence? "Do you know the name of the agency?" She was smart, and she knew there were ways to get out of an abusive relationship. Maybe hiring me was the first step on that path. I'd leave counseling her to get out until after I closed the case, because if she wasn't ready to leave, no one could make her.

"McCarthy Family Unity Corp." Glenda asked me to hold on for a second.

In the background I heard Nora ask for juice, and Glenda respond. Then a drawer closed, and she was back on the line. "I have the card. Alan needed me to sign some documents, and they came with our representative's information. I never met the man, but Alan talked to him a lot. It was the owner, Viktor McCarthy. With a K."

"Send me a picture of the card," I said. Maybe I could talk to Viktor with a K. "I'll let you know when I've talked to your husband."

We ended the call and a moment later I received a text with the card. Very helpful. Phone numbers, email address, and website. I had something to look at before I called Alan. Something that would give me credibility for the cover story.

I started with the website; nothing spectacular, probably a free template and it was more like a brochure than a portal to their business.

Mr. Viktor McCarthy's picture was on the about page. It wasn't a full body picture, but he had that tall person look. Red hair, the really white skin that goes with it. Freckles, wide cheekbones, bright blue eyes. I could have been describing David, but no, there was something in Viktor's expression that felt fake.

I put in a call, just a voicemail and a woman with an Australian accent telling me it was full. I debated not going to their office for all of three seconds. It was dangerous to leave a hole that big in my backstory for Alan.

The office wasn't downtown, which I expected, but in Kitsilano. Annoying because it was unlikely to be near Alan's. I would need my car, and I would be on the road all day.

I dressed in my most professional black pants, white shirt, and black jacket. Not a suit, but it looked like one. My car was parked a few minutes' walk away at The Bayshore Hotel, and it would take me anywhere from a half hour to an hour and a half to get to McCarthy's office.

IT WAS in a fairly new condo building. Offices on the street level, apartments above. Squeezed between a yarn store and a day spa, the office wouldn't hold more than the receptionist, Mr. McCarthy, and a client. Interesting.

"Mr. McCarthy isn't in today," the receptionist said. "I can make you an appointment for tomorrow?"

I wasn't waiting for tomorrow to start making progress. But I didn't need to talk to the boss for my purpose. I checked the nameplate on the desk.

"I don't know, Cynthia. I'm not looking to adopt, really. My client is. I was hoping to talk to Mr. McCarthy so I can make a recommendation."

"Oh, well, I have some literature here," she said, picking up a folder of fact sheets. "I might be able to answer your questions."

"I was hoping for some referrals to satisfied clients." I took the folder. "The people I represent are very wealthy and leery of choosing the wrong company. You know how rich people can be."

"I do, but I can't give you any names beyond what are in there." She pointed to the folder again. "They gave their permission to be used in our material."

I guess I didn't really need to get Alan's name from here, and pushing was going to cause problems. "Would you have their contact information?" I flipped open the folder while she considered.

"I can't give you that," she said. Now her voice had gone from friendly and helpful to flat and suspicious.

"That's okay, I'll manage. Thank you so much, Cynthia."

I left my card to prove I'd been there, but I had what I needed. The first name on the testimonials page was Alan Blackhouse.

10

I called Alan's office and he agreed to meet me there at eleven. It would leave me the rest of the day to follow up on whatever I got from him. And I wouldn't be playing tag all day long.

It was downtown, in a shared office environment. Odd for a financial planner, but maybe he spent most of his appointments in client locations. What did I know?

I dropped my car off before heading down. It was a fifteen-minute walk, and parking would either cost me a month's food budget or would take too much time to find. Being on foot made me much more flexible.

The address was at the corner of Homer and Pender in an older building. The elevator was out of order. Alan's office was on the fifth floor of a six-floor building. The stairwell was carpeted and had a musty smell, but nothing truly egregious. I was struck with the feeling that if I was looking for someone to advise me on how best to invest my savings, I would look elsewhere.

The shared office space was newly renovated; polished

concrete floors, walls painted a gray so pale it might as well have been white. The desks were light wood, clean design, and from what I could see, in good shape. The chairs had seen better days. There was a receptionist. He looked up and gave a smile. "Are you looking for space?"

"I'm meeting Alan Blackhouse," I said.

"Yes, he booked an office." The guy stood and pointed to a small room in the back of the open space. "He should be there now."

I thanked him and made my way in. Only a couple of desks were occupied with head-phoned people intent on their screens. I doubt they even knew someone was walking past. I knocked on the door, and Alan opened it, ushering me in before closing the door behind me.

He was good looking. Graying hair, smile lines around his eyes, a short well-trimmed beard, a rigid posture that was probably trying to disguise his stature. This close, it didn't work. He was about five six. Shorter than me.

I should be feeling reassured by the warmth of his greeting, but those smile lines could have come from something other than kindness, and that posture could be arrogance rather than insecurity. I wanted quite badly to leave the door open, but that would put him on alert that his usual charm wasn't working. And maybe his charm worked on regular clients.

"Please, sit." He pointed with an open hand to the one client chair. "Can I get you water? We have coffee if you'd prefer."

"No. I'm just fine, thanks. I hate to rush this, but I have another appointment in an hour."

"Of course, we both have far too much to do to sit around," he said. Taking the chair on the opposite side of the desk, he steepled his fingers and looked at me like I was the only person in his life. Creepy.

"As I said on the phone. I'm looking into some adoption agencies and your name came up. My clients are very anxious to bring a child into their family. Can you tell me your experience with McCarthy?"

"Did you get my name from him?"

"From the brochure. You gave them a testimonial, or is that not legitimate?" This early in the interview, I had to keep control, so if I answered a question, I needed one to throw back at him. "You did adopt a little girl through them. Or am I mistaken?"

"Our personal life is not your business, Ms. Deacon."

"I suppose it's not that important. You were a client, and you can still give me your impression. My clients are willing to expedite the process if that's a possibility. Don't want to offer a fee if the service isn't available, of course."

"You mean pay for a kid?" Alan sat back now, relaxed. He'd tried to sound offended, but it came across as greedy. He wanted a cut if money was changing hands.

"That's a crude way of putting it," I said, all offended. "We are aware that being able to pay certain fees will speed up the process. Once they have been approved, of course."

He rocked back in his chair. "Are you a cop?"

Did he really think he was being entrapped? Whatever he'd done, the cops would find out if they knew to look. "I am a private investigator. My client has no interest in bringing the authorities to the table."

"I don't think I should tell you the details of our adoption," he said as he leaned forward again.

I'm not sure I would have trusted the chair to hold me with all that movement, but it didn't collapse, just creaked.

"Then, I should move on to other names on my list." I stood and looked at my phone like I was checking a list. "Perhaps your wife is willing to help another woman become a mother."

"No." He stood and leaned across the desk. "Leave my wife out of this. She's delicate. I arranged the adoption. She knows nothing about it."

I looked at him like I was thinking about his words. Too soon to fold. "My clients are not interested in upsetting anyone, but they do want a child. If you refuse to answer my questions, I need to move on. Your wife is on the list of people I need to talk to until I get what I need."

The idea I had a list finally seemed to get through. It wasn't so much Glenda he worried about now. There was a name he wanted to keep me from reaching. Good.

"Look, yes, I paid for the adoption facilitation. That's what Viktor called it. A fee. Gets the paperwork completed fast. And can tip the decision in your favor. If your clients are worried they won't qualify, Viktor is the right guy."

"So yes, paying for a kid works." I couldn't help but throw his words back at him. "Do they do any diligence? On the family or the child? My clients don't want to adopt anyone who is, shall we say, less than perfect."

"They check to see if you've been caught abusing or selling the kids on when you go to them for a kid. Some contact with the police takes care of it. They showed us the family history for Nora. You'll get a quality kid."

I had to leave before I threw up all over his rented desk. Whoever he thought was on my list was scary enough that he wasn't worried about me turning him in. He just had to keep me from calling the next name.

"Thank you," I said. "I will pass that on. My clients will be happy."

I didn't wait for him to say anything more. As soon as I knew Glenda and Nora were safe from retribution, everything I had was going to David and his buddies in the RCMP.

11

I went home after meeting Alan. I'd used up the only lead I knew enough about to work. Now it was time to wrap my head around the things I'd learned. Should I report the adoption agency? Yes, but not now. Should I let Glenda know how the interview went? Also yes, but I needed to decide what to tell her. It was mostly supposition about his current criminal behavior. She could wait to hear that Nora's adoption might not be valid and might not stick. I'd let her know before I told the authorities so she could make some decision about Nora's future.

Then my phone rang. David. Another problem to think through when I had time.

"Hey."

"You met with the Blackhouse guy," he said.

Shit!

"You're checking up on me? Am I being followed?" Attack first has worked in the past and it was my go-to approach.

"Not you, and it's not me." I heard the sigh as he tried to get his exasperation under control.

It took a second or two for this to sink in. If it's not me, then Alan Blackhouse? Not David, thank whatever ran the universe. Then who? It could be any number of local and foreign acronyms. But only a few who would call David.

"Who is watching him?"

"You need to talk to the RCMP," David said. "They want you to stop, but I wasn't planning on being their messenger."

"I don't have to talk to anyone," I said. Childish, but I was just stalling. They might not have a legal right to pull me in, but that didn't mean they couldn't get in my way.

"Don't count on it. Charity, I'm trying to keep you from being arrested for interfering with an investigation. And you knew the RCMP was on a case, so it might stick."

"I'm not getting in their way. If they wanted to, they could have stopped me before I went in. If they're watching him, they probably have a tap on his phone."

"I didn't ask if they had a warrant, Charity. It won't hurt to talk to this guy. I know him."

It would hurt if they told me to stop face to face. I needed wiggle room. Whatever they were looking at Alan for, they wouldn't be concerned about Glenda and Nora.

Did I trust David's assurance? Yes. But I also knew he shouldn't be making any promises that someone else was going to have to keep.

"I can't leave my client out in the cold," I said. "She needs my help and there's a kid."

"Then meet Andy."

"If I don't walk away from the meeting, you need to warn Glenda." Every instinct I had screamed at me to avoid it. But David wouldn't set me up, and he was too smart to be used like that.

"Why do you want to protect her? She lied to you, and Val might have paid the price."

I wasn't interested in digging into my psyche. "Because she wants to know what her husband is up to. If she was involved, we wouldn't be having this conversation because I wouldn't have the case."

"Okay. What if the meeting was in public?"

He was trying to get me to do the right thing. Not only the right thing, but the sensible thing. His question made me wonder if I was being paranoid. Did I really think the RCMP would drag me to jail for refusing to back down? No. If they really wanted me to stop, they'd be at the door. It didn't mean they were going to pat me on the head and tell me to continue with my little case. They wanted something.

"Okay. Tomorrow morning. Eightish. White Spot on Dunsmuir. He's buying breakfast, and just him."

"Good. I'll introduce you and leave," he said. "You'll listen, right?"

Geez, was I that difficult to deal with? Okay, yes, when I wanted to be, I was a bitch.

"I'm not going to let him push me around, but yes. I'll listen." And I would because you never knew where a lead could come from. "Are you coming by tonight?"

"I'll pick you up at seven-thirty tomorrow," he said.

That wasn't an answer. "Are you coming back?"

"I'm on a big case, Charity. I'll be back when it's done. A few days, maybe more."

I said goodbye and set my alarm for the morning. I had a few things I could dig into from Alan's interview, but not enough to keep me from worrying that I'd screwed up with David.

Before I started looking deeper into the adoption agency, I called Glenda and told her I'd met with Alan, and I had no news. She didn't press me for any details.

Maybe she was regretting hiring me. Or maybe Alan was

home. But he should still be out giving investment advice, or whatever he actually did for a job. And she would have ignored my call if she couldn't talk.

I wasted a bit of time wishing for a way to find out what warrants had been issued that included Alan Blackhouse's office. But if there was a register, it was tightly locked from outside access.

So far, I had a dodgy adoption business, a link to a bar where gangsters hung out, and some unspecified federal case. Tomorrow I'd try to get information on the last piece from this Andy guy. I wasn't ready to go hang out in a gang bar — it was way too early in the day. I could dig into Viktor with a K and see if there were any indications that kids were being sold for reasons other than just rich people hopping a line. If there were, I'd call David right away. But I didn't think Alan would risk Glenda being dragged into that kind of cesspit. She struck me as the kind of woman who'd give the cops anything and everything she knew if kids were being hurt.

And she didn't know Nora was bought.

And Nora was happy.

If I acted too fast, Nora could go from a happy and safe-ish home to the foster system where she could encounter anything from disinterest to abuse. And yes, there were lots of great foster parents, but there were lots of bad ones too.

12

I was waiting outside for David five minutes early. No need to add to his frustration with me over unimportant things like being late to a meeting. He was right on time of course. I tried not to think of it as a reprimand.

The good thing about getting downtown this early, a few parking spaces were available across the street from the White Spot. I headed to the restaurant while he dropped a couple of coins in the meter.

"Wait up," he said, jogging in behind me. "I'm supposed to introduce you, remember?"

"I wasn't going to wander around the restaurant asking every man sitting by himself if he was waiting for me." I nodded to the hostess and waited for David to talk.

"We're meeting Andy Miller."

She stepped from behind the stand and led us to the back of the restaurant. One man at a table, one that had chairs and a bench seat. In his early fifties by the look of it. He stood to greet us, and I noticed he was short and stocky, but comfortable with it. He had that kind of face that right now looked friendly, but all it would take was a frown and losing the smile to make me want to back away before I got hurt.

David introduced us and then left.

"Are you hungry?" Andy asked, pointing to the empty bench seat. He sat again and pushed a menu toward me.

I preferred a chair, easier for me to leave if I just had to push one back. The bench seat was cloth so no quick slide to escape. I got in anyway and grabbed the menu.

"I'm not sure I'm staying long enough," I said.

A waitress stepped up from around the corner. "What can I get you?"

I ordered coffee.

She was back in seconds with my mug and a top up for Andy. "Let me know if you need anything else," she said before returning to her real station. This section wasn't really open. Andy needed privacy.

"What did David tell you?" Andy asked.

"You want to talk to me. You are surveilling my client's husband. I assume you want me to walk away and leave everything to you." I picked up my coffee and sipped to stop me from barreling ahead with all my accusations. I'd promised to listen.

"We are working a case on a very big individual. Your client and her husband are part of that investigation."

"Who? Maybe I can stay out of your way if I know who you're targeting."

"No. I am not going to tell you that."

Why didn't he just spit out his orders and let me get on with my day? Because I wasn't going to back off.

"Then, what will you tell me?"

He leaned back and looked at me with the angry face on. Then he grinned. "You're right. The best thing for everyone is if you back off. The guy we're targeting is harming a lot of people, and if he gets away..."

"I'm not arguing against catching the bad guys," I said. "My client has nothing to do with it as far as I can see. I don't want her becoming collateral damage."

"I checked on you."

"You did what? Am I being watched?"

He waved his hand to dismiss my worries. Did he think that would work? "No. Just asking around to find out what I can expect if we try to stop you."

I couldn't say anything. He was right. It was reasonable to check out the person you were going to battle. Because that's exactly what it felt like. "And?"

"They said you wouldn't stop. But they also said you were unlikely to outright lie. That you were very good at finding the truth, and that you were stubborn enough to run headlong into trouble but smart enough to ask for help — sometimes not at the last minute, too."

He must have talked to a lot of people. Mostly things I was proud of, and none of it wrong.

"Okay, so you know you can't shut me down. Why are we meeting?" Now I wished I'd ordered bacon and eggs. My idea of a quick fight and then storming out was blown.

"A couple of things. You need to know that whenever you are interacting with Alan Blackhouse, there's a good chance you are being recorded."

"So, you know about the adoption?"

"Not from you. We don't have a bug in the office. We already knew from a different source. Another team is looking into it."

"Glenda doesn't know. Do I need to warn her that some-one's going to take her child away?"

He looked at me over his mug and then shook his head.

"It doesn't work that way. If the kid is in a good home, no one is going to take her. Is she? In a good place?"

"You tell me. All I have with Alan is the adoption and a good feeling he's shady."

"And the wife?"

"She is the one with the suspicions. Nora is fine with her. Don't you have the house bugged?"

He hesitated. Deciding if he should tell me?

"We don't have a warrant for the house. Just his cell," he admitted. "But the cell is always listening unless he knows to turn that off."

A pretty narrow warrant. "And does he?"

"Not always." Miller smiled. "So, can we trust you to be careful?"

"As much as I can," I said. "I still need to find out what he's up to. Unless you want to tell me and then I can end my case."

"Nice try. Look, we think it's money laundering, but so far, we can't find proof. If you can get him to talk about that where we can hear, I'd be grateful. I don't think you'll have any more success than us. But you don't need solid proof. You just need your client satisfied."

That was true, but knowing that the RCMP would be listening made it easier for me to take risks. And if they found their proof, I wanted them to share. "Maybe we can work together?"

That made him laugh out loud. "I doubt it, but keep asking."

I wasn't getting anything else from Andy, so I thanked him for the coffee and headed out.

13

Knowing about the adoption and the probable link to some crime boss made me anxious about Glenda. Yes, I keep telling people, even myself, that she's innocent, but all I had was a gut feeling based on a meeting, a phone call, and the ability to discount her behavior when Val went missing. And the authorities agreed, as far as I knew. None of the actual cops could tie her to the gang. Or, maybe, they were keeping that bit of information from me.

When I called, she'd said to meet her at home for lunch. Alan would be gone until later and it was safe to talk.

If he dropped in, my cover was the same. I never promised that I wouldn't speak to Glenda, after all. So now I stood on the sidewalk thinking through how to ask my questions. If she was innocent, I didn't want to get her involved in something big enough for the RCMP to investigate, and if she was part of the problem, I needed to leave the house fast and call Andy.

The sun filtered through the leaves of the old trees; wind sent a whisper through the branches. All peaceful and sleepy. It made me suspect that the world behind these heritage doors was more real and hard than the outside showed.

I marched up the stairs and before I knocked, Glenda pulled open the door and ushered me inside. She took a peek at the neighbor's house before closing the world out.

"The street was empty," I said.

I meant it to reassure her, but it did the opposite to me. I cursed Andy and David for winding me up so tight I worried that I needed witnesses to me entering the premises. They were both responsible for me second guessing Glenda.

"Coffee?" Glenda asked over her shoulder as she led me to the kitchen. "I can make you a sandwich and you can join Nora for lunch."

"It's probably better if I don't interact a lot with Nora. We don't want her telling daddy about the lady who visits her."

"She doesn't talk to Alan that much. She's usually in bed before he gets home," Glenda said. "They eat breakfast together, but she's more interested in talking to him about her imaginary friends."

Was Alan avoiding his daughter now she'd been paid for?

"Let's hope he'll think I'm one of them if she does mention me." I settled on a stool at the kitchen counter and pulled out my notebook. Nora was in her corner at her own kid-sized table, poking at a bowl of baby carrots and chewing on a peanut butter and jelly sandwich. She looked up at me and smiled, teeth covered in peanut butter, white bread, and purple jelly mush. Delightful. I gave her a smile and finger wave and then turned my attention back to her mother.

"I found a few leads," I said as soon as Glenda stopped

fussing with the coffee. "I don't have anything solid for you. Can you give me some more details about why you think he's doing something behind your back?"

Glenda sipped her coffee as she thought. I hoped she was thinking of a way to help me and not a way to lie to me.

Nora started singing something repetitive about a shark. Hummingbirds flitted past the kitchen window to a feeder. I expected some animated bluebirds to come tweet around our heads.

"This is more than just the usual. I mean the usual you see in fiction or on TV. Yes, he works long hours. I can't always get him on the phone. I wonder if he's taken a shower before coming home for some reason."

"The more?" She was right, none of those things guaranteed a problem at all, and only adultery if anything. No hint of serious criminal activity.

"He has his own accounts," she said. "When we got married, he said we should open joint ones for expenses and savings but keep our own ones for spending. He said we can buy surprise presents that way."

"That's pretty normal."

"I know. When I worked, I kept my income as spending money, but then Alan convinced me that I didn't need to keep my job and I quit. I was a marketing specialist, and it didn't take much convincing. After that, the funds from the business flowed into the joint account and then our separate spending came out. Now he transfers money to the joint one from his. I still get my spending money, and I don't need to scrimp, but I have no idea how much he's keeping back."

I made a note. She was right. It sounded exactly like a way to protect money prior to a divorce or to hide a lot of extra income, or gambling debts, or a drug problem. Or the price of an adopted child. Too many things it could be. I needed to look at his finances to try to pin down what it actually was. "Did you ever ask him about the change?"

She glanced at Nora, who was using her crayons. "No." Then she turned to me. "Look. He's never hit me or Nora. I wouldn't put up with that. But I've seen his temper turned on other people. Some questions are not worth the risk."

A way to explain her complete lack of knowledge of his crimes. "You think this is about more than just hiding money, right?"

"He isn't planning on divorcing me," she said. "I would know."

She sounded certain, but there were plenty of ex-wives who'd thought the same thing. "Do you have the paperwork around the adoption?" His finances should be there, but with a shady operation, who knew what diligence they did.

"They are in a safe deposit box. I can scan them and send you a copy. But not today."

"As soon as you can," I said. I had other ways of getting the information, but it would be enlightening to see what Viktor thought constituted good business practice. "I'm going to start following Alan around. He knows who I am, but I'll be discreet. If he asks about me, I need you to do two things. First, say I did come to ask about the adoption agency, and you sent me away."

"Your cover when you met him? Yes. I can do that."

"And I need to hear about it as soon as it's safe to tell me. If he has a temper, I need a heads up that he's caught me."

"Yes. I promise."

I headed back out not convinced that she'd told me everything, but much less paranoid about being played.

14

I had enough experience to know that the worst thing I could do was run off chasing Alan around without any intelligence to follow. So, setting up searches and analyzing the information I got was the extent of my afternoon's work. Boring, but at least snacks were within reach, and the opportunity to sit on the rooftop patio to be distracted by the sails of the boats around me. I also had a view of the other floating homes in my neighborhood. Most people were at their jobs, and only five of us have houses here, so there was rarely anyone to chat with during the day.

By evening, I was tired but had a couple ideas of where to find Alan. Not only in the day when, if he was smart, all I'd find was him giving financial advice. No matter how shady his clients were, that wouldn't move me closer to closing the case.

What did I have that might satisfy my client? A list of places where he hung out at night. Not usually tonight, but tomorrow night, a good chance of finding him at a suspect bar out in Burnaby. *Sila*; the best place to meet dangerous and rich Russians.

I packed up my laptop, glass and plate to take them into the kitchen. One more glance around the neighborhood and I saw David strolling down the finger dock. Was I forgiven? Or was he coming to pass on some order from Andy Miller? My guess was the second.

I opened the door just as he arrived. "Hey, should I call for pizza?" Of course I had no groceries to make dinner. David would be aware of that.

"Let's go out," he said. But not like a date night event. Like he figured I would behave like a rational human being in public kind of thing.

It wasn't worth trying to get him to stay. And I told myself I'd be a good girlfriend and listen to him. I wouldn't yell with witnesses around. And if we had a fight, I could grab a cab. "Where? Do I need to change?"

"You look fine," he said. "Nothing fancy. Maybe somewhere in Gastown?"

The restaurants in the neighborhood ran from a small sushi stand all the way up to five star, depending on where you chose to start in Gastown.

We took his car, which I interpreted as an indication he was still miffed — well, that and the silence. Otherwise, we would have walked and enjoyed the evening.

He parked in a lot and when we were standing on the sidewalk, I asked, "How bad is this going to be? I mean, is it *The Old Spaghetti Factory* bad, or should we just head over to *Pourhouse*?"

"You mean how well behaved do I expect us to be? We don't need to worry about that. How about *Nuba*?"

"Can't go wrong with Italian," I said.

We were seated and waiting for our wine before I pressed him. "So, am I forgiven?"

"Charity, I'm still annoyed with you. But I think it's going to be kind of normal for us in this relationship. I know you didn't give up on the case. I know you aren't working with Miller. I think you're getting in over your head."

Wine for me, a Coke for David, and a basket of focaccia with a dipping plate made it to the table before I asked anything more. I relaxed a little because now I could stall by eating and drinking. It gave me something to do other than reacting badly to whatever he said. With that thought, I sat back. Why did I assume I was going to react like a kid in a tantrum? I had no answer, so I pushed the thought to the corner of my mind where I put everything I didn't want to deal with — like everyone does.

"Miller won't let me investigate. He'll expect me to do only what he tells me, and if the situation gets tricky, I'll be sidelined."

He didn't respond so I filled the silence, even though I knew I should stop talking and wait him out.

"There's definitely something going on that might hurt my client." I picked up a chunk of bread, dipped it in the oil and vinegar and stuffed my mouth to prevent me from continuing.

David looked at his soda, turning the glass in his fingers. Then he looked back at me. He was serious, but not angry; he couldn't hide anger on his pale skin. "I'm annoyed at myself more than at you. I should never have thought you'd back off and stay safe. I was wrong to expect you to."

This time I kept quiet.

"Knowing you are capable of dealing with your cases and acting against all my cop instincts to protect people, is a battle. What did you learn from Mrs. Blackhouse today?"

I chewed another clump of bread to damp down the flare of anger. I needed to get help on handling my feelings with something other than food before I gained a ton of weight. When I finished, I asked calmly, "How did you know I met with her?"

He laughed, which was both annoying and a relief. My pause had worked.

"The RCMP are watching the house. Easier to get a warrant for that. Saw you go in, and about three minutes after you left, Alan came home."

I almost choked on my wine. "Glenda said he would be out until dinner. Did he see me?"

Our food arrived before David answered. The waiter offered cheese and pepper and then withdrew.

My gnocchi smelled delicious, David's Osso Buco gleamed with richness.

"He wouldn't have. You left before he drove up. They'll text me if he leaves."

My appetite came back with the assurance. "He isn't usually home in the day. Glenda told me we would be fine. I did have a cover story though."

"And if you worked with Miller, you wouldn't have to risk it. They could warn you."

The gnocchi was as tasty as the aroma promised. I put a spoonful on David's plate, and he gave me a bite of his meal. I preferred mine. "I guess that ship sailed."

David concentrated on his food, but I saw a smile emerge. Damn him, I'd been handled. Oddly, it didn't make me want to lash out.

"He'll meet with you tomorrow."

"Jerk," I said with a laugh. "Can you join us, at least to start?"

He agreed and we settled in for our meal.

When we headed back to the car, we walked arm in arm. "Are you staying over?"

He gave me a squeeze. "Yes."

15

Back at the same White Spot and the same table in the back. This time I ordered breakfast in the hope we'd have a conversation, not a battle.

We talked about small daily stuff until our food arrived, Andy had two kids and a wife. His mother sat on the council in Haida Gwaii. Interesting, and whether he planned it or not, the details made him a person instead of a uniform.

"So, what am I doing here?" I asked. "Are you going to tell me to back off again? Didn't work last time, so what's new?"

Andy smiled but David tensed. He was expecting something like that to happen. I guess he didn't trust the RCMP completely either.

"I did some more research on you," Andy said. He buttered his muffin and didn't look up. "You must be very good, or very, very lucky."

I had nothing to add, mainly because I feared it was the second and that luck could run out with no notice.

"You also won't back off," he added. "Why aren't you some kind of cop?"

David snorted a laugh at that. I jabbed him in the arm.

"I don't like rules. The last time I worked closely with the authorities, I felt like I kept running into walls. And everyone expected me to rebel but wouldn't let me have any scope to do my job."

"And you did rebel, right?" He gave me some time to answer, but I just stuffed a forkful of potatoes in my mouth. He smiled. "Look, I think we should work together. You get results and you don't break any serious rules."

Perhaps I hadn't found one yet.

"What do you mean work with you?" David asked. "Charity is quite capable of solving her own cases."

Wow, he was really surprised at the offer.

"I think he means just my case," I said. "Yeah, I can provide Glenda what she needs. In fact, I can do that in the next day or so."

"Are you going to use her as bait?" David asked him. "It's too dangerous."

I looked at David trying to figure out what was going on. "Last night you wanted me to work with them."

"On your case, maybe a little intelligence on Blackhouse," David said. "It helps you and them. The big one, no. Crime like that is their business. You aren't trained."

Weird. When I thought he was protecting me in the past, I couldn't stop the angry response. And then he actually wasn't doing it. Now? He definitely was and I wanted to hug him. Love is confusing. I leaned in and kissed his cheek, leaving a little grease mark.

"It's okay," I said. "I am not going to be bait." Then I remembered all the times I'd put myself in that position. "I mean, I'm not signing up to be bait. But if I can help, I'm on board. You already know how I work, so you have fair warning."

"Good," Andy said. "I have some stuff on Blackhouse, more than the adoption thing. I need to know if the wife is involved."

"I don't think so. She's looking for a way out. She doesn't know that he paid to adopt the kid. She could be an asset, I guess. My gut says he's kept his activities completely separate from his home life."

"I need more than your gut to convince a judge to issue a warrant or use her. I'm going to give you some information about him. You need to talk to the wife and get a clear answer. If she doesn't know about this, she's likely not involved."

"Enough that she will get away if she uses it against the people you want?" I dropped my napkin on the remaining food on the plate. Knowing I could get Glenda the proof brought up the idea of how dangerous it would be for her to use anything I found. "Or do you want her to sit on the information?"

"You want her to agree to being monitored," David said to Andy. He turned to me without waiting for the answer. "Better and faster than a warrant, and they will protect your client, Charity."

Andy nodded.

And it would be further proof she had no part in whatever the RCMP was investigating. And it might close his case quickly, which meant fewer people hurt in the long run.

"I can be there when you talk to her," David said. "If she has any questions. And another opinion that she's innocent will help."

I needed to see the evidence first. "No, I'm not bringing a stranger to the meeting." Glenda must be able to feel safe. She knows me and only me. "What have you got?"

Andy retrieved a folder from the seat beside him and

dropped it on the table, then placed his hand on it. "Our target is Ivan Kuznetsov. We think Alan is one of the people doing his money laundering. We haven't been able to access his records yet, but my guess is Ivan is his only client and any names on the accounts will be fake."

It didn't make any sense given the office Alan used. Perhaps that was just for me or other civilians he pretended to help. Kuznetsov had shown up a few years ago, and suddenly the random gang killings stopped. Like someone was running all the organized crime in the city. The thought triggered my memory about Guy's warning. No. It was like the local gangs were scared to say no to someone.

"And what do you want Glenda to do for you?" If this guy was as bad as they thought, Glenda could be in danger just being married to Alan. "I still haven't seen anything I can use."

He flipped open the folder. Three pictures. A tall man in his fifties, balding and hard-bodied, and even in the slightly blurred surveillance photo, his eyes looked dead. In all three images, Alan stood beside the guy; no doubt that he was part of whatever was going on. "Kuznetsov?"

Alan nodded. "We want your client to give us access to Blackhouse's files. Nothing more. When that's done, we'll move her and the kid to a safe place."

I know I should trust that a big organization like the RCMP would protect Glenda. But I didn't. Mistakes happen. Cops take bribes. I would make sure to get Glenda secure and able to look after herself no matter what happened. "I'll talk to her, today. I need some time to prep."

Andy pushed the folder to me. "Use these. Tell her who Kuznetsov is. Call me when she's ready to talk to me." He stood and took the bill to the front.

"Charity," David said.

"I know. I'll be careful. I promise."

16

One day an investigation that ran smoothly from one clue to the other would fall into my lap. Of course, in that scenario, there'd probably be no reason to hire me. As much as I insisted to Andy Miller that Glenda was clean, his questions created a worm of doubt. I'm not gullible, but there's always a blind spot, and it was different with every client. Until I was sure I wasn't being played, I needed to go deeper into Glenda's past.

When I took on a new job, I did check some background, but mostly to find out if they could pay me, and if they had a real problem. A couple of clients had tried to hire me to frame someone. Now, I made sure my cases were legit.

Going deeper entailed checking her phone history. Looking at the older transactions for suspicious activity, and basically looking for evidence she wasn't lying rather than confirming she told me the truth. An important difference in perspective. Glenda had already lied, so I guess I was actually looking for proof she wasn't lying again.

I called my friend at the phone company to pull her call and text data. He reluctantly told me it would come in an hour, reminded me if he got caught, I'd be going down with him, and then assured me he was too good to be caught. He always came through, but only after trying to weasel out of the job. When I say friend, it's a stretch.

Her banking transactions only showed the money coming in from Alan's account and withdrawals for items like food, kid's stuff and clothing. No cash taken out for an untraceable payment. No suspicious deposits. Alan wasn't using her to launder money. Or he was better at his job than I was at mine.

I pulled a credit check to see if there were any other accounts or debts. Secret loans might mean anything, but usually nothing innocent.

No unexplained cards or loans, but the report listed an account in Nora's name. Interesting. Before I pulled up the information, my phone rang.

"It's Terry."

You'd think someone who works for the phone company would understand caller ID. "I know. What do you have for me?"

"I'm sending you the call, text and location data for her mobile. I couldn't find any other cellphone under her name, but they have a land line."

"That's getting rare, but can you forward me anything on that?"

"It's in the husband's name. So, yes, but someone else asked about that number. And his cell."

The RCMP. They'd been denied the tap on the home phone. If I had Terry send me the file, would it trigger an alert? Probably, and I didn't want another meeting with Andy. "Just hers will be fine."

"I took a peek, not much going on. You want me to reach out if we get another request?"

The phone company must have a flagging system for official requests. Or Terry was the only person working there who leaked information, so he made it his job to learn about anyone poking their nose into records.

"Yeah. And can you tell if she opened an account with another provider?" I crossed my fingers.

"No." He paused for long enough that I wondered what he was holding back.

"Really? Or you do have the information, but the company is not supposed to because of privacy laws."

"I don't have access to anything like that. We officially don't even look for the customer details on the competition."

If she had another phone contract, it would have shown in the credit report, or if it was a burner, in her credit card or banking statements. "Okay. Let me know if anyone asks about her account."

"Will do. I gotta go."

He ended the call and my computer pinged with an incoming file.

Twenty minutes later after looking at every data point, plotting out her day and trying to find something incriminating, I gave up. She barely went anywhere other than the grocery store. She didn't call or text any burner phones. The fact I could gather that information in such a short time told me one of two things. Either she was exactly what she seemed, or very good at hiding her activities.

If I let this consume me, I would never solve the case. The only concrete evidence I had was her lying to me about meeting Val. The easiest way to resolve that was asking her outright why. I don't know where the reluctance came from, but I should have done that sooner. What would I do with her response? Maybe that's why I didn't ask. And now I was hip deep in the case, so the answer had to be nothing. So, no point in asking.

The time I spent produced some results; I may not have a list of clues and actions, but I did find information. In a case, information was more valuable than truth about something in the past.

Time to set up a meeting with Glenda and show her the pictures. That was my job, not tricking her into confessing something for the RCMP.

I pulled out the photos again. If this was my proof Alan had stepped into dangerous territory and Glenda should run, I wanted to be clear about how I would present the implications to her before I made my move.

Alan sitting with the local Russian mob boss — allegedly. Alan next to the same clearly menacing man — although I wasn't sure the danger showed in the photo. Alan in a club at a table with Ivan and a couple more hard-looking men. Why couldn't one of the pictures reveal a gun, or Ivan killing someone? If they had, I'd be out of a job because they'd all be in jail awaiting trial, and Glenda would have the proof she needed. The gray areas were what created my business.

I texted Andy for the name of the club. Bingo. There had been three shootings there in the last month. Glenda might be convinced by the location, if not the people in the photo.

The photos were timestamped — evidence needs those kinds of details. Alan out and partying between one and two a.m. might be enough for her anyway. My contract involved a spouse acting suspiciously, not gang activity. I tried to burn that into my brain. Going outside the parameters of my job could get me killed this time.

As much as I wanted to go to the house, I had no excuse. And dropping in risked Alan finding out about everything. So, I decided to call Glenda, but not from my house. I needed stimulation. Especially after such a frustrating waste of time on the computer. And Stanley Park was only a few blocks away.

A walk around the entire seawall sounded like a great idea when people talked to me about living in Coal Harbour. "Oh, you live so close, I bet you do the seawall all the time." Yeah, no. Who has the time to do a two- or three-hour trek with few opportunities to exit? I strolled to the park and picked a bench about ten minutes from the entrance. Sunshine, kids running around, the occasional Frisbee crossing my field of vision, perfect.

"Hello," Glenda said. She knew it was me because their home phone had caller ID. So, Alan or someone else must be with her.

"Is it okay to talk?" She could call me back if she said no.

"Yes, just a moment." She put me on hold.

I waited, breathing in the smell of the water and... was

there a popcorn vendor around? No. A girl on the next bench picked pieces from a brown paper bag; brought from home.

"Charity?" Glenda sounded more herself.

"What was that about? Are you okay?"

"Alan was leaving. I told him you were one of the other moms from the play group."

"Is he likely to check the recent calls and see my name?" One of the downsides of a land line. You couldn't delete information.

"I'll unplug the phone for a while. The memory will clear. If he asks, I'll say a bunch of spammers disturbed Nora's nap."

Smart woman. "I think I found that proof."

"You can bring it now," she said.

I was not taking a chance that Alan would drop back for something he forgot and catch us. "No. We should meet outside the house. Can you get out for coffee?"

I heard Nora in the background, chatting away with no pause for anyone to answer. A nice little fantasy world where she was queen. What I was going to show Glenda might bring that crashing down. Glenda still hadn't answered. "Are you still there?"

"Sorry. I can't come out today," she said. "I have to meet Alan for a client event."

Maybe the photos wouldn't be a surprise after all. "What kind of event?"

"A fundraiser for rescue animals. One of his biggest clients is on the board."

And maybe he only showed her off at safe parties. It meant he had legitimate business, or the 'client' was just faking it. "Tomorrow?"

"If you really think I need to come out. Tomorrow, lunch.

Nora will join us. I don't want Alan to know I went out without her."

"Is there a place you usually go?"

"I don't go out enough to have a usual place." She chuckled when she said it, but my instincts were hearing all kinds of alarms.

"Does he keep you in the house? Does he beat you?" No point in being coy and letting her hide behind subtle questions. "You need to get out if he's violent."

"No. He has a temper but knows better than to turn it on me or Nora. My world revolves around Nora right now. When she's in school, I'll have time for coffee dates. We should probably do this away from New West anyway."

Every answer she gave sounded reasonable, and every single one of them tripped alarms. "Why?"

She laughed again. "Maybe no good reason, but if we go out for lunch and then Alan takes me for dinner and the server says something like nice to see you again..."

"I'd say that was a long shot, but life is full of them. Okay, how far?"

"Less than an hour away," she said. "I know this is business, but it will be fun to have a day out."

There were a few communities near her that would work, but I remembered the location of the club I'd found in my research. "We should go east," I said. "How about Port Moody?"

It was a smallish place, and not on the main run as you go that direction.

"Okay, do you have a restaurant in mind?"

"Brown's?" A chain was the best way to keep a low profile. Independent restaurants were great, but less busy and more personal attention.

"Can you give me anything now?" she asked.

Telling her part of the news wouldn't help her feel better and would deprive me of the chance to observe her reaction. Because every time I thought I'd convinced myself Glenda knew nothing of Alan's activities, she said something that made me suspicious again. Like all this fear about Alan finding out. Yes, it could be about him stopping her leaving, but she'd just denied he had a violent nature.

"I need to explain it," I said. "What I have is not something like catching him with another woman or robbing a bank. Context is important here."

A long pause while Nora chattered in the background again. I waited her out.

"Tomorrow then. One?"

"Perfect. Call me if anything changes. And be careful."

"I always am," she said before hanging up.

I let a minute pass before calling back. The phone was out of service. She'd unplugged it to erase the memory on the caller ID.

What did she mean when she said, 'I'm always careful'? More red flags popped up. Most of my cases didn't make me waver like this. Yes, I sometimes had to figure out the truly bad guy amongst a bunch of shady characters. But I don't remember a time when I worried so much about the client. I blame Andy and his RCMP suspicion for making me paranoid. I leaned back and let the sun warm my face and tried to let it go.

My phone rang. I looked at the screen. Andy, like I'd summoned him.

"Yes?"

"I need an update."

"It's been less than a day and there's nothing to report."

"Did you use the information yet?"

"Tomorrow. Look, don't call me for updates. I'll let you

know when I have something. This isn't the kind of thing you can just dump on someone."

"This case is important, Charity. Things move fast."

Yeah, so fast you need me to help out.

"I'll call you after lunch and tell you what I find out. Don't interrupt my process."

He snorted and ended the conversation. What happened to the reasonable guy who convinced me to assist the mighty RCMP?

18

I got to the restaurant early and took a table with a bit of privacy. Having someone close by would make it impossible for me to control the situation. If she reacted badly to the pictures, I needed to make sure we weren't bothered by other customers offering help to the distressed woman.

Glenda arrived ten minutes late, Nora in tow. When the kid noticed me, she ran to the table. "I can draw you a new picture."

I smiled at her and didn't know what to say. Kids were not my thing.

The waitress brought over a highchair — something I should have thought of earlier. Glenda put her daughter in and dug a pad of paper and crayons from her huge purse.

"She'll be quiet now," she said. "Should we order?" She nodded to the server.

"Something fast," I said. I wasn't here to chat, but the pictures and the identification could wait while we did the social things. Maybe a little build-up to the reveal would help her believe what I was about to show her.

While our meals were prepared, she fussed over Nora; wiping her face, brushing her hair back and asking questions until the kid put down her crayon and said, "Mama, I am busy drawing."

We both laughed and then our food arrived.

"I guess I'm nervous," Glenda said. "I'm paying you to find out the truth, but now that you found something, I'm hoping it was all in my head. It's stupid, right?"

"Food first," I said. "What did you tell Alan about being out today?"

"I said I was taking Nora shopping. He won't want any details," she said. "Nora, eat your lunch, please."

Nora gave her mother a glare before picking up a baby carrot and crunching it with attitude. Apparently, her art was more important than food.

"What will she be like as a teenager?" I asked. If they didn't check her attitude soon, no one would survive when the hormones took over.

"We're working on it. You've seen her when she's not in a snit, that's most of the time. When we get between her and her drawing, this happens."

"Maybe art school?"

I kept my attention on Glenda. I didn't have any more direct questions about her involvement with Alan's business, but how she spoke about the family could tell me a lot more than a lie. She said 'we' when she talked about raising Nora. There were no plans to leave Alan no matter what she learned today. I'd assumed she would do that if the news was bad, but maybe not. Women stayed with men they couldn't trust all the time for all kinds of different reasons.

"You haven't been around kids much," she said, stroking Nora's hair and earning a sigh. "Tomorrow she might start obsessing about dolls, or Lego or some TV show."

How careful was Glenda? "What if she tells Alan about me?" I asked my voice low in case little ears were perked up.

"I'll say an old friend called," she said. "I know someone who will confirm if he wants proof. But he won't."

"And how much is Nora likely to tell him about what happens?" I imagined her reciting everything. *Daddy, a lady was waiting for us in the restaurant, and she showed Mama some pictures and Mama cried...*

"She won't say anything. She's shy around him, and when he gets home, I'll make sure she's down for her nap."

Was it my concern how Glenda dealt with the news? How she managed to keep Alan from learning what she's done? Only in as much as I needed to protect myself. But I had people to help me. She was alone. Her husband made sure of that.

"What are you planning to do with the results?" I couldn't push away the idea I would feel guilty if anything happened to them. It wasn't my business, but guilt didn't much care about those kinds of details.

"I don't know," she said. "Until I see what you found, I can't plan, can I?"

"Do you need anything else?" The waitress appeared at my side. I'd eaten on autopilot.

"Just coffee for me." I didn't want her hovering until we paid the bill, and I couldn't eat another thing. This way we'd be left alone for ten minutes or so. Plenty of time.

"Do you have tea?"

She rattled off the teas, Glenda chose Earl Grey and then looked at me. "Are you saying I should expect the worst?"

Nora was still drawing and humming a song I didn't recognize. A glance at her artwork reassured me Alan wouldn't learn from Nora's work that she'd been with me. The page bloomed with butterflies and flowers.

"It might be." I watched her reaction. A slight tightening of her eyes, but nothing else. "I need to explain what you are going to see. It's not graphic, but the implications are bad."

"So not another woman. At least he's not boring in his betrayal." She sat back as our drinks were put on the table, then thanked the waitress. "I appreciate your concern. If this is as awful as you are hinting, I will disappear with Nora."

Did she know someone who could make that happen? "It's not so easy to do nowadays," I said. "With the right contacts, Alan or someone involved can find you."

"Do you know anyone who will help me?" The lightness had gone from her tone.

"We can talk about what to do after I've explained." Andy better be prepared to protect these two. Because Glenda wasn't faking. My gut knew that, and I trusted my gut more than the RCMP. "You aren't in danger just because I found proof."

"I understand. Nora and I are in danger, though. Have been all along?" She didn't wait for me to confirm. "Whatever it is didn't grow out of me feeling insecure. In fact, that was the thing bothering me underneath, right? It made me worry about Alan and hire you."

I nodded, waiting to see where she would go. Up to now, in my mind she was a victim. Someone I needed to protect. I was wrong. Yes, she needed protection, but she wasn't afraid — of whatever she thought Alan was doing, or of seeing the proof.

"Yes. Because you hired me, you have options. Before that..."

"My world would collapse with no notice."

"Yes. What do you know about the Vancouver criminal world?"

19

"Nothing." She put her hand on Nora's leg to stop her kicking the table. "I mean, only what's reported in the news."

"The worst criminals stay away from the press." I placed the folder with the pictures on the table but didn't open it. "They run the gangs."

"And Alan is one of these *Godfather* types? I don't believe you."

Not a surprise. She'd been expecting something a bit more mundane. "No — maybe. But he's been socializing with one, possibly more."

"He isn't... I don't think he knows anyone who lives that kind of life."

When Nora started humming, Glenda touched her leg again. At least she wasn't getting up and taking the kid home.

"But you aren't surprised he's into something criminal?"

The waitress approached from behind Glenda this time. I shook my head and thankfully she didn't slap the bill on the table.

"I thought maybe embezzlement," she admitted. "I know that's not a victimless crime, but it's not violent. He works with people's money and the temptation is there. And he changed the way our finances worked..."

I wanted her to come to the conclusion herself so when I showed the pictures, she wouldn't need much persuading. The end result here was to get her and Nora safe before the RCMP case blew their lives to pieces. And I'm pretty sure I would need to sell her on taking Andy's help. "When people handle a lot of money, and have a weakness, they can become involved in something they can't escape."

"You think someone threatened him?"

She was very calm, maybe for Nora's sake, or shock, or she knew all along. I couldn't keep that little voice satisfied that she was innocent.

"Maybe, or they said they'd hurt you. These people need someone to manage their finances too."

"Money laundering? Yes, Alan would know how to do it."

"And how to create the system?"

"I suppose. Opening accounts?"

Fake portfolios would be a good way to launder the cash at the end of the process. Someone needed to get the money to him first. "More than that. These systems are shut down all the time. Would Alan be able to figure out how to set up a whole new way to clean dirty money at a high volume?"

"I don't know enough about how the legitimate investments work, but Alan is smart. I thought he had a better moral compass than this. You brought proof?" She nodded to the folder.

"I have photos of people hanging out," I said. "Not actual crimes. The RCMP have evidence the one man is a big mover in the local gangs — all of them. I believe them, but they don't have hard evidence, yet."

I expected her to ask for the pictures. But she just stared at the folder. I guess it represented the last step. If she never looked at them, everything was a possibility. As soon as she saw her husband with a known gang boss, she couldn't deny anything.

"You want me to provide proof?" she asked. "I don't think I can."

I'd never considered using her like that. She wasn't a good candidate for that kind of work. Her life was too constrained. Her daughter needed more attention than an undercover operation would allow. And she might be cool with me, but I didn't represent danger.

"No." I would make sure Andy didn't plan on it either.

She let go of Nora's leg and put her elbows on the table. Her gaze locked onto the folder. "Show me. Maybe I know this man. Maybe the police are wrong."

I couldn't blame her for holding out hope for it to be a mistake. I hated to be the one who shattered it.

I flipped open the cover and placed the photos on the table. I let her look without comment for a few minutes. Let her tell me if she knew Ivan.

"This man?" She pointed at Ivan in each picture. "He's the one the police are trying to get proof on?"

I nodded, worried if I started to explain, she would never reach the point that she accepted the facts.

"This club," she said. "Isn't it that where those shootings took place?"

The interior of the place had been splashed over the front pages a month ago. "Yes."

She stared at the images again. I let her take all the time

she needed. Nora was in her own world, crayons and carrots mixed together on the high-chair tray.

"I don't know any of these people. And none of this is proof Alan is doing anything wrong."

"This is what I have to show you," I said. "The RCMP have more. Would it help?"

"If they don't have enough to arrest him?" She glanced at her daughter. "How will more of this kind of thing convince me?"

"I can get the head of the investigation to meet with you," I said. "I get this is hard. You can't let Alan learn you've seen this. No matter what you decide after seeing their evidence, these people are dangerous."

"I wish I'd never called you," she said, leaning away from the table. "But I did, so I can't stop now. If Alan is guilty, he needs to face the consequences. If he's not? He has a temper, and I don't want to take the brunt of it."

"I'll call my contact in the RCMP."

"Why do you believe this?" she asked. "You've only been on the case a few days. Something convinced you."

Good question. "This isn't the first time I've seen this kind of thing. People caught in something they can't get out of without losing something they hold precious. People able to hide their true nature." *And I trusted David—and maybe Andy a bit.*

"Okay, call this contact." She turned from me to fuss at Nora.

I'd taken the precaution of letting David know where we were meeting. With luck, Andy was close.

"Miller," he said when he picked up the phone.

"She wants to meet you." I could be as terse as he was.

"At her place. The husband is tied up in North Van. How quick can you get there?"

Why at the house? Oh, yeah. If Glenda gave permission, they didn't need a warrant to bug the whole place.

"An hour? Will that be soon enough?"

"If that's the best you can do, sure. He's going to be a while over there and we can always find a way to delay him so we can clear out."

20

I followed Glenda home and parked on the block behind the house. I hoped I'd catch sight of Andy, or the people watching the house. I told myself that he would call if we were in any danger. The fact he hadn't meant Alan was still occupied.

The watchers were good. I didn't notice anyone lurking in a car or loitering. The trees still had enough leaves to hide the house, so I didn't expect to catch a glimpse of a lens in a neighboring window.

I was about to open the gate when Andy and David turned the corner. Why was David here? Too many people, too much risk. It was still nice to see him.

Andy cocked his head, signaling me to go ahead. I guess three people arriving at once might draw attention. And if we were right about Alan and Ivan, the RCMP might not be the only people keeping an eye on the house. Why did I have to get those revelations after things might have gone too far? I knocked on the door, trying not to look around for other observers. Glenda pulled it open and ushered me in.

"How long before they arrive?" she asked. "Nora's down for a nap. She won't wake up, but..."

"Alan is being watched," I said. "We're safe."

She pointed to the kitchen and then peered through the peephole, like it would help her see what was going on.

I was halfway down the hall when she let Andy and David into the house.

The introductions and offers of tea and coffee didn't take much time. Glenda settled us down in the living room. She and I sat on one sofa, David took a chair and Andy the facing sofa. "I can hear Nora better. If she wakes, I don't want her seeing you."

"We should probably get to business," I said. "Andy, show her what you've got."

He'd been busy. He laid out the pictures I had on the coffee table. He added printouts of phone calls or texts. "Ms. Deacon already told you who this man is," he said, pointing to Ivan. "These transcripts are conversations between Kuznetsov and your husband. Take your time. Ask whatever questions come up. We'll receive notice if Mr. Blackhouse is on his way."

Glenda stared at the amount of paper on the coffee table. She didn't pick anything up, and she didn't try to read the contents.

I picked up one sheet — Alan talking about a shipment. Even when they thought no one was watching, they were too smart to say money laundering.

"Start here," I said, passing Glenda the record. "It's pretty clear they have a relationship."

She scanned the paper and tossed it back on the pile. "But not anything illegal, not for certain."

Still not convinced he was as much of a bad guy as we told her.

"The shipment they are talking about," Andy said, pulling another photo out of his briefcase.

The image was a shipping container. In the back, five very young women huddled together, eyes wide, dressed in rags and dirt.

"How can you be sure?" Glenda's voice shook.

He turned the image over so we didn't get drawn to stare at the misery pictured there like people slowing down to look at a car crash.

"We placed a trace on your husband's phone. Not the one you know about. He has a number of pay-as-you-go phones. He's not as diligent as he should be about hiding his activities. This container was at the location in the first conversation. Your husband's burner phone was there at the same time."

She looked at me. "You said money laundering."

David picked up another photo but kept it face down. "The investigators think Kuznetsov is trapping your husband deeper into the organization. It's a way of ensuring his loyalty."

I took the paper from him and peeked. A dead body. A man, a good suit, around Alan's age by the look of what they left of his face after putting two holes in his head. I handed it back. Glenda didn't need to see that level of brutality when it might end up being Alan, or her, next time.

"So far, he's managed to keep you and Nora from being dragged in," David said. "We need to stop him before that changes."

Glenda's breath was ragged, and she'd wrapped her arms around herself.

"Do you still think Alan is innocent?" I asked. Clearly, Andy wanted something more than permission to bug the house.

"Nothing here is really proof," she said. "I'm not saying he wouldn't be tempted to dabble in some gray areas, but violence and people trafficking? I can't reconcile that with the man I married."

"If we had evidence like that, we would have arrested him. Yes, we found enough to bring him in, but not enough to keep him. I need more to make arrests." Andy piled the photos and transcripts together and put them in his briefcase. "We want your help."

If I had seen the proof before this, I would have done things differently. Glenda needed to get away fast and be protected. Alan might not hurt her or Nora, but Ivan Kuznetsov wouldn't hesitate. I'd dealt with people traffickers before. This is what Guy meant when he warned me off. I didn't care what happened to Alan. He'd earned whatever consequences were coming. Glenda had done nothing wrong.

"What do you want her to do?" I asked. "You're not just talking about a few bugs in the house anymore, right?"

"We need you to set a trap," Andy said. "We'll be watching everything. You won't be in danger."

"No, you need to protect her," I said. "You lied to me. I would never have agreed to do it this way if I knew. David, I trusted you."

"I didn't know about this either, Charity." He turned to Andy. "Something changed, right? This wasn't the plan when we arranged to meet."

So, Andy was the only one who lied to me. I didn't know how to pull Glenda out of the situation. She needed the RCMP for the level of protection turning in a dangerous man like Ivan Kuznetsov required. They wanted a reason to use the resources on that. If she was willing to set up her husband, and testify, then the plan would work. There was no going back, but I still didn't like it. And Andy would get an earful of my feelings about his actions later.

"Glenda, it's too late. Whatever changed puts you and your daughter in danger."

"Andy, what did change?" David asked. "You can't hold back if you expect her to put her life and her daughter's life in peril."

He definitely didn't want to tell us. Then he checked his watch. "I can't go into a lot of detail. We don't have the time, and more knowledge puts Mrs. Blackhouse at more risk."

"More danger?" Glenda asked, finally getting mad, not scared. "No. Not knowing the truth or knowing only part of it is worse. Stop talking about me while I sit here. I'm not stupid. What changed? What exactly do you want me to do?"

"There's a shipment of weapons coming in," he said. "They are planning something big, maybe a takeover. These are missiles, ammunition that can punch through armor plating. We need to stop the sales before someone starts a bloodbath."

Silence.

What would I do in Glenda's place? No question, I'd help. But I didn't have a kid. And I'd been in danger before.

"What do you need me to do?"

Andy's phone chirped. He read the text. "Shit. Alan is here."

21

"Here? We have to get out." I looked at Andy like he would know what to do. If I was alone, I wouldn't do that, another reason not to work with partners. And why was I looking at him for help? It was Andy's fault we didn't receive any warning. It didn't matter right now. I could talk my way out of the situation and keep Glenda safe without two men sitting there acting like they were up to something.

"No time," he said. "I'll deal with it."

I looked at Glenda. She was shaking but her face still had color. David stood and started for the door. To intercept Alan? That would just make everything so much worse.

"No. You follow my lead. I'll use the same cover as before. I'm here to talk to her about the adoption agency — Alan knows I'm on that case. You and Andy are my clients and you're worried about the cost and want to make sure it's not a scam that takes your money and still leaves you without a kid, or one so damaged you can't help them. Well, any more of a scam than selling kids to good homes."

David turned on his heel and rejoined us. "Andy, scoot

over. We should sit together." There was a reason I... felt strongly about him.

The back door clicked as soon as he sat.

"Glenda?" Alan called, walking into the room before she could answer. He stopped dead, his face flushing when he noticed she wasn't alone. "Why is she here? Who are they?"

I stood, hoping his temper wouldn't keep heating up. Nothing of the helpful businessman remained in his expression. And a worried dad wouldn't be boiling with all that anger without someone triggering it. "I asked your wife to meet with my clients."

"You should have come to me. I told you Glenda had nothing to do with the adoption."

"David and Andy are less interested in the process. They want to hear if you experienced any issues with Nora. Since Glenda is the primary caregiver, she's the best choice." I struggled to keep my voice even. He wasn't the only one with a temper and mine triggered when someone tried to control me.

"Yes," David said. I turned to see him holding Andy's hand. "The money isn't the problem. We want to make sure that the kid isn't... well, you hear stories, don't you? About nightmare children and then you are the bad person for trying to return them."

"Nora is healthy, and that's all you need," Alan said. "I'd like you to leave."

"We haven't had a chance to talk to your wife," Andy said. "I know you think it's okay, but I'm sure Mrs. Blackhouse has more details."

"Yes," David said. "You work long hours, right? I'm sure the child is fine when you see her. I'm going to be the one staying at home, so I want some assurances."

"There's nothing wrong with Nora." Alan took another step into the room. "I said she was perfectly normal."

The situation was escalating, and I couldn't think how to change it. I didn't want to leave Glenda here alone with him in this mood.

David stood, then Andy. The testosterone level went through the roof. I might not have a plan to deescalate, but I knew this confrontational attitude wasn't going to help. But Alan backed up the step he'd taken into the room. Andy and David remained where they were. Okay, maybe they knew their stuff. Maybe all that training made a difference.

"I understand," Andy said. "It's difficult when someone questions the way you are raising a child. We didn't mean that at all. Let's keep our voices down so we don't wake Nora, that's her name, right?"

"Yes," Alan said. "How did you learn about Viktor?"

The change was abrupt enough to make me suspicious. Was he going to check? "I don't think that's important," I said. "You must know how to reach him. Who referred you?"

Wrong question. Alan glared at me. This time his face paled. His fists still clenched, but I didn't think the tension came from anger. He was scared. And angry.

Andy and David remained still, maybe getting ready to defend us?

"If the person I'm thinking about sent you, you know better than to question his advice." Alan flicked his gaze from the men to Glenda and to me. "You need to leave. Now. My wife isn't going to talk to you."

Not now for sure. I picked up my purse. "Well, I think we've learned what we came for. Gentlemen?" *Please go with this.*

Andy turned to me and nodded. He put his hand on David's arm and steered him to the front door.

Glenda followed us and let us out.

"Are you going to be okay?" I asked as quietly as I could. Alan hadn't come to make sure we left, but he was probably close.

"I'll be fine. I'll call when it's safe. Then you can finish telling me what you want me to do."

She closed the door and I walked away.

"We aren't going far," Andy said. "Out of sight, but ready to come back. He won't stay home for long."

"How can you be sure?" Now that we were out of the house, I needed to burn off the adrenaline. "Let's walk around the block at least."

"He needs to make sure Kuznetsov didn't send us." David took my arm. "He won't ask directly, and he won't do it on the phone. But he can't risk Ivan finding out that he kicked us out of the house if we were friends with the boss."

"Good thinking on the cover," Andy said. "He bought that part."

"Thanks, I think," I said. "Is someone still watching the house?"

"Yes. Until we can get a few bugs in there, we can't pull the observers." He checked his phone. "They'll text when he leaves. I need to update the rest of the team so we can try to backstop the adoption story. I'll let you know when you can safely return."

"Like your other guys did? If they can't keep track of him, what good are they?"

Andy kept his eyes on his phone. "I'll find out the details after we've resolved this problem."

"We'll stick close," David said, drawing me away. "There's a coffee shop around the corner."

I hoped Andy was right. Until I saw Glenda safe and

unharmed, I wouldn't be able to breathe normally. If anything happened to her, it was my fault.

22

The coffee shop sat on a rise and gave us a view of the bridges and water. The tide was turning so the surface looked like pounded metal, and the current was outlined in the ripples and tiny eddies. A few logs floated free from a boom upriver. Some tugboat would be out soon herding them into a safe area to be collected.

The peace of the scene did nothing to ease my fears. Every second that passed before I could check on Glenda was time for Alan to drag out the real story.

"I think he guessed you were cops," I said to David. "I don't think we fooled him."

"He's never met us," he said. "We aren't in the public eye, there is no reason for him to suspect. Besides, I think Andy and I did a good job in our covers."

They had, but it didn't mean they got away with the story. "He already suspected me, I think. I should never have agreed to talk at the house."

"And Glenda wasn't going to stay out of the house any longer," he said. "It was hard for her to stay with you when you promised she would only be out an hour."

"He smelled the cop on you," I said. Then, because I realized that might sound wrong, "I mean the aura of authority. What if he's in for the day?"

David didn't answer for a moment. Long enough for me to drag my eyes away from the tiny boat cruising on the river. He glanced at his phone and then up at me. Then he put it on the table. "I know what it looks like when a cop's cover is blown. I did undercover for a while. One gig was enough for me to be completely sure I couldn't do the job. I had the skills; I didn't have the drive to be away from friends and isolated in a world of criminals."

"Did you catch the guy?" Bitching about something we couldn't control, like Alan, wasn't getting anywhere. A bit of David's history should take my mind off my worries. "Or did someone blow your cover?"

"We got her, and she still doesn't have a clue it was me. I saw another UC make a mistake, and the look on the gang members' faces changed in an instant. One second he's one of them, the next they were planning on how to kill him. And he knew it."

"What happened?" I guess I should trust his judgment of Alan's reaction now that I had some context. I was trying to, but blind faith didn't work for me, and it was going to take a while because screw ups like this kept the distrust alive.

"He got out before they could settle the plan and never came back. I heard he left the force." David looked at his phone again. "He was maybe ten minutes away from dead. And I'm pretty sure the gang leader planned to make me pull the trigger."

"To prove your loyalty?"

"To make it so I couldn't get out. So, yeah, her form of

loyalty. Alan doesn't suspect us of being cops, but he didn't fully believe us either."

"We should have brought her to my place," I said, not quite ready to let go of the idea that we didn't need to be in that house.

"Maybe, but think back to how your conversation went in the restaurant. Would she have convinced herself we were wrong if she had the time?"

"She was still in denial," I said. "She wanted to hear what you had on her husband, but she thought there would be an explanation. So, maybe. But I thought Andy wanted us at her home so he could wire the house as soon as he got her."

"Partly, but he wouldn't put her or you in danger just for the sake of a few hours delay. We all thought it was the best move while Alan was tied up with something an hour away. We should have been warned in plenty of time."

"So, someone dropped the ball. How did he get home without anyone knowing?"

"I'll ask those questions after we make sure your client is okay. And still willing to work with us."

"That's what Andy said. And if she's changed her mind?" Glenda was so close to the edge of believing us, and now Alan had his chance to sway her.

"If you trusted me, you wouldn't ask that. It doesn't matter if we lose her as an asset. The fact Alan slipped his tail is a serious breach. We'll find out."

This trusting business was tricky. I didn't mean he would just walk away. Whatever the official line, David would do his best to help Glenda. "I do trust you. I meant if she isn't willing, is there anything we can do to protect her?"

"Not much. Protection requires a cooperative subject. We have no way to force her to be careful. She doesn't know enough to totally blow the case, and I didn't peg her as someone who would side with the criminals."

"Me neither. Maybe I can take care of that." I glanced out at the street. People walking and driving at a leisurely pace. A mainly residential area, low speed limits. But it was the most obvious way out of the neighborhood for anyone heading downtown or east. "I won't risk anything, but I can't walk away."

"Convince her to work with Andy," David said. "It's the safest thing for her and the kid."

No argument from me. As much as I didn't remotely trust him, the RCMP was her only refuge.

A car passed at speed, one I knew from my research. "That's him."

I grabbed my bag and started for the sidewalk. David held me back.

"Let's just wait a minute," he said. "If he's gone out to pick up something from the store, we'll be caught again and with no way to explain."

I pulled out of his hold. "We'll walk slowly."

He took his jacket off the back of the chair and followed me out. When we reached the sidewalk, he paused. "Andy's on his way. Half an hour at most."

"Text him that we aren't waiting," I said. "I'll go in alone if you don't want to come."

He rolled his eyes at me. "Already done. I'm right behind you."

23

We got to the corner before Andy sent a reply to David. I'd try not to add that to the list of grievances. Perhaps he didn't know about including more than one person in the thread. "He wants us to wait," he said after reading the screen.

"No. We might not get much time," I said. We weren't running because speed drew attention unless you were wearing more spandex than really necessary. "If he did something, we need to know. I won't leave Glenda there to deal with the fallout of Andy's mistake."

David stopped. I didn't want to go in alone, so I did too, pulling him under the shade of a tree. The canopy was great for hiding us, but its ancient roots bucked the sidewalk so badly it was an obstacle course — another reason not to run.

"We need to be sure he's not out on a quick errand," David said. "If we go back now, it might make things worse."

"He doesn't strike me as the kind of guy who runs out for milk," I said. "And he was definitely headed for downtown."

"Or around the block. He might be checking to make sure we aren't going to come back."

I wanted to tell him he was wrong, and our covers worked. That Alan didn't suspect the cops. I even opened my mouth to say the words. But I couldn't speak. If he was right, Alan didn't need an excuse to be suspicious of us. Anyone who worked with a criminal like Ivan Kuznetsov would be paranoid, or dead. And if I was right, we had no reason to rush back and save Glenda.

"Andy must have a way to check," I said, nodding at the phone. "Ask him."

"I did. Be patient."

"I can call Glenda." I dug out my phone, but David stopped me before I hit her number.

"He might have installed a wire on the land line." He checked the street, probably looking for Alan's car, or a nosy neighbor. "He's had time to bug the entire house."

"Then it's a good thing Andy didn't have time to put any devices in place. What if he'd already done it? Heard everything we said? Maybe that was why he came home." No way would our covers survive him hearing the earlier conversations.

"Andy was sure we were okay, or he wouldn't take the risk." He didn't look at me, like he regretted taking Andy's word.

"He had time to do a lot of things."

And Glenda had time to tell him everything, and he has a temper, and he's probably scared all the time that he'll do something Kuznetsov won't like.

I fought to stop myself from running to the door to check on them. "I can knock on the door, pretend I'm there to apologize. She can send me away if it's a problem."

David's phone pinged.

"Andy. He says Alan's on the freeway."

"No need to delay; I'm going," I said, stepping out of the shade.

"We are going," David said. "Keep your eyes open for anyone who might be watching."

The street was empty. That didn't mean no one was looking. If we couldn't pick out the RCMP observers, then we wouldn't see any others who might be keeping watch. That fact didn't stop me scanning the houses and sidewalk as we approached. No twitching curtains, no one coming out for a walk all of a sudden. I still felt eyes on me.

I ran up the steps and knocked. No one came or called out.

I knocked again. The door was thick, and even when I put my ear to it, I couldn't hear anything. The window beside it had a privacy film or something on it.

"I'll check the back," David said. He left me at the door waiting.

I sent a text to Glenda, but she didn't respond. Not to worry. Maybe she'd gone upstairs to check on Nora. No need to panic.

David rejoined me. "I can't see anything. Most of the windows are too high. Good security, but shit for surveillance."

"I'm picking the lock."

"Give me a minute to make sure it's safe."

"I know you can't do it, but I'm not a cop. If you need deniability, you can walk around the block." I would be inside by now if he wasn't around.

He shook his head as he looked down at his phone. "I'm letting Andy know something is up. Maybe they saw her leave and no one told us. He can obtain a warrant so we don't mess up the case."

More delays.

I had my picks in my hand. The lock wasn't complicated.

David moved to the corner of the porch when his phone rang. I told myself I'd deal with the fallout later as I slid the wrench in and started jiggling. I wouldn't open the door. Just get it ready.

"What are you doing?"

Shit, I should have given his call a bit of my attention. But lock picking isn't something you do with half your concentration.

"I thought it would help to prepare. The door is still closed."

"He's calling for a warrant."

"Can we go in based on my worry about her wellbeing?" I knew if I went in without permission, I was breaking and entering. And I wouldn't ask David to lie for me.

"We need something more."

I turned the handle and let the door pop off the latch. It didn't open all the way but would only need a nudge to do so. Nora began crying long, sobbing wails.

"Is that enough?" I asked. I pushed the door wider.

"Kids don't cry like that for nothing," he said, pulling me away from the door. "I'm going first."

I let him. He had the training, not me. Even without his weapon, which he'd left locked in his trunk, he was more capable of dealing with whatever was going on.

"Stay out," he said, coming to a stop. "I need to protect the scene."

I didn't leave, but I didn't go farther in. Nora was screaming for her mother. Glenda was lying on the floor, not responding, bleeding.

I stepped back to the porch. "I'm calling Child Protection."

"Good idea," David said. "Andy's people will be here in a couple of minutes. I've called an ambulance."

24

I was on hold with Child Protection Services, so I tucked my phone into my shoulder and joined David, who was saying something to Glenda.

"I've got her," I said, sitting on the rug next to her. "Can you help Nora?" I had no skills with kids even when they weren't freaking out. He had brothers and sisters and nieces and nephews. He must have learned something.

I touched Glenda's neck. A pulse. She wasn't dead yet, and if the ambulance came fast, she might survive. As to recover? The damage looked too bad for me to be hopeful. Her hand was warm, so I held it gently. If she could respond, she only needed to move her fingers.

"Glenda, we're here. You are going to be fine. Nora is fine. Just hold on." Not even a twitch of recognition.

David lifted Nora and faced her away from her mother. He whispered to her while stroking her back. She still screamed, but the volume seemed to be a bit lower.

"I'll take her to the kitchen," he said. As soon as he took one step, Nora started kicking. "Okay, we'll stay. I promise we won't leave your mom alone here."

The hold music on my phone stopped and a woman's voice told me her name. I gave her all the information we had. It was going to be an hour before they arrived.

"We'll stay," I said. I needed to be off the call and concentrating on Glenda. The woman on the phone seemed happy that David was a cop and didn't tell me to call family or friends or anyone else to take the kid.

"If we hadn't come here..." I couldn't finish the sentence aloud. In my head all the accusations screamed to be spoken.

David started that bounce parents use to ease a child into sleep. "You don't know we caused it. The attack might have happened anyway. No. It would have happened. Maybe not today, but this? Inevitable with a guy like Blackhouse."

"Not we," I said. "Andy. He should have left it to me. I would have had her away from Alan before this without sparking a fit of rage."

"Andy didn't do this," he said. His words sounded reasonable, and I had a hard time keeping my temper up when he didn't fight back. Then I looked at him and saw fury. He might not say he blamed Andy, but he didn't think this was on Alan's agenda for the day either.

Glenda was still breathing. I squeezed her hand a little, trying not to add to her pain, but she gave me no response. Her face took most of the punishment, but now that I heard her breathe, I figured she'd taken some damage to her ribcage. He'd used his fists and the leg from one of the kitchen stools. Thank God it was wooden, probably the reason she survived. The hall table was broken, but the pieces were all accounted for as I checked around. The rug was pulled up in places. Blood splattered the ceiling and walls.

"Where is that ambulance?"

"Coming," David said. "It's only been a few minutes since I called. That's them," he added as sirens wailed closer.

Nora wasn't screaming any more, but hiccups and gulping sobs were worse.

"He should have left it to me," I said again. "Andy should have let me talk to her, get her okay to bug the house. She was ready to agree."

"You can't blame him," David said. "He's trying to stop Kuznetsov and a lot more of this kind of thing happening."

The logic didn't pass me by, but anticipated violence on strangers was different from seeing my client in a pool of her own blood on the floor. "I could have stopped this one incident."

He closed his eyes and bounced Nora a few times before answering me. "You can't be sure of that. Different circumstances and it might be both of you lying in your own blood. We aren't the reason he did this."

"I don't blame you," I said.

"Thanks, but the only blame here is for Alan Blackhouse." He'd said the name at a whisper. "This was going to happen no matter what you did. He chose to become involved with Kuznetsov. He hid everything from his family. They had no choice. If she knew what he was doing, she could have left. She was going to leave."

I couldn't be sure of that. Yes, she'd agreed to help, but only because she thought we were wrong.

"She still deserved protection." I gave her hand another squeeze. The sirens passed us by. "She's going to die before they get here."

"We can't move her."

"I know. It's hard to wait, though. I don't want to do more damage by moving her, but I feel like I should be doing something."

He took a step toward me, still bouncing Nora who'd stopped wailing and now whimpered between hiccups. "What does Glenda's breathing sound like?"

It was so quiet I had to lean in close to her body. "Steady, but there's a squeak."

"Her pulse?"

"The same as before. She's alive. I know moving her will make things worse. I wish I could make her comfortable. It's best that she's unconscious."

He stepped away from us again and looked over his shoulder at the kitchen. "Is there someplace I can leave Nora? She's asleep. Worn out from crying."

"Put her on the couch," I said, nodding toward the living room. "If Alan didn't tear everything apart."

He looked in and then entered the room, returning without the kid. "The room is fine. She'll be down until someone disturbs her."

I heard another set of sirens approaching. "Help is coming," I said to Glenda. She didn't respond, but if there was a chance she could hear me, I wanted to keep her comforted. And it made me feel like I was doing something.

He bent over and looked closely at Glenda's face. "I don't think the damage is as bad as it looks. Lots of blood, a broken nose, but her jaw looks whole."

"I guess this will get Andy his warrant." And I had a lead to follow — this kind of violence didn't happen once. Alan had done this to someone before.

"Alan won't come back here," David said. "He might not survive Kuznetsov finding out about this. Too much attention from the wrong people."

Footsteps on the stairs made me turn. Andy and another man. No ambulance yet.

25

"You need to leave now, Charity," Andy said. His tone was so reasonable, like I'd been waiting for permission from him. "We'll take it from here. Your job is done."

"I'm not going until Nora is safe. And Glenda is in the ambulance. She is my client."

"The kid needs us to hang here," David said. "We won't get in the way."

"You can stay, Anchor," the other man said. "It's a crime scene. No amateurs."

David touched my arm and I refrained from yelling when I said, "You made this happen."

The ambulance arrived before anyone could respond to me. A pair of EMTs ran up the stairs, a stretcher held between them. The woman told us to move and surprisingly Andy didn't argue. The man was already checking Glenda's condition.

"Living room," David said. "Nora's in there sleeping so keep your voices down." A good tactic if he thought we couldn't fight it out in whispers. I would not let the RCMP get in my way. I was right to suspect Andy of using me and Glenda. Why did everyone think I was paranoid when this kind of stuff happened? The cops were just as bad. Not David or Leigh, but the rest of them.

"Who's this guy?" I asked. Keeping my voice low didn't make me any calmer. But it did let me hear the EMTs doing their jobs.

The newcomer stood in the doorway like he could stop me from leaving the room. Tall, blond, mid-fifties, built like a retired wrestler, he formed a good barrier. I wouldn't let him stop me if Glenda needed me, no matter how tough he thought he was.

"This is my supervisor," Andy said.

The man held out his hand. "Michel Benoit."

I really didn't want to shake his hand. It seemed like I was giving him control by doing it, but I wasn't going to be childish. "Charity Deacon, the woman in the hall is my client."

I noticed David didn't need to be introduced.

The male EMT came through the doorway. "Who's the contact for Mrs. Blackhouse?"

"I am." I gave him my card. "Are you taking her to Royal Columbian?"

"No. VGH has the capacity. It'll be a while before you can see her. They'll probably get her into an OR pretty quick. There's some internal bleeding."

"I'll check on her," I said and slipped past Michel to watch them take Glenda out. I locked the door behind them. If Alan came back, it wouldn't help, but that's what cops are good at, taking down assholes. And I had three of them sitting in the room behind me. Cops, not assholes — maybe.

"Now what? Are you going to give her some protection?

It won't be hard for Alan to find her if he's interested." If I kept talking, they couldn't argue.

"On the way," Andy said. "We need her to testify."

"You need her to survive," I said. "She can't set the trap now, so what are you planning to do?"

Michel finally sat. I guess he decided the lurking at the doorway didn't intimidate me.

"We'll bug the house," he said. "Maybe Alan will come back and feel safe enough to say something if his wife isn't around."

"We'll figure out a new way to get Blackhouse, and we'll turn him," Andy said. "What he did to her means he's scared."

"What you set him up to do," I said. "If you'd left this to me, Glenda wouldn't be in the hospital. Her daughter wouldn't be on her way to a foster home or group home. Alan would be falling for the trap."

I waited for someone to stop me. No one did. David kept his eyes on Nora. She was still asleep, but any time voices raised, she moaned a little. Andy and Michel didn't even blink. They were letting me run out of energy. Like I was a disgruntled teenager.

"I'm going after Alan," I said. "I'll let you know when he's ready to be arrested."

Michel sat back on the couch, relaxing. "No. This is an RCMP investigation. You will not interfere."

If he thought I'd be reasonable, he hadn't done his homework. "Unless I do something illegal, you have no choice."

Andy wasn't looking at his boss. Maybe he was in trouble for bringing me in. I couldn't dredge up any sympathy. He left Glenda high and dry. And me for that matter.

"You have been helpful," Michel said, "but now you

need to leave it to us. We have the authority and the resources. Your efforts to turn Alan Blackhouse are appreciated. We don't need another disaster like this."

David's hand clamped down on my arm, but I ignored it. This guy was trying to blame me for what happened, and I couldn't let him get away with it.

"This isn't my doing," I said. The words hissed out as I tried not to wake the kid. "Your people screwed up. If you want to help me, then we do things on my terms. If you don't want me involved, then I'll work on my own."

The doorbell rang and David hurried out to answer it. Coward.

"We can always charge you with interfering in an investigation," Michel said.

"And I can always tell the press that you are strong arming me, and that you caused an innocent woman to put her life on the line without the proper protection." I wouldn't. Going to the media would kill my reputation for discretion, but he didn't know that.

"Child Services," David said.

All the arguments stopped while we went through the process of handing Nora over. Andy went to the nursery and packed a case for her. I wasn't leaving the room until she was gone. When the woman asked for the father's information, I said he was unavailable, and David used his badge to support my claim that I could be listed as the contact for any problems.

It took no more than fifteen minutes of Nora making a tired attempt at fighting to see her mother and struggling to stay with me, and finally getting worn down again. The childcare people were patient and murmured assurances until Nora relaxed enough to strap her in the car seat. I watched from the doorway, not taking the chance they'd lock me out.

Andy stood behind me, Michel was poking through the house looking for evidence, and David stood with the social worker.

"Don't push too hard, Charity. I will bring you back on the case, but Michel is freaked out about the situation. I know how to calm him down. Losing Alan was big, and now we have to investigate this incident because it's related to organized crime. I'll have to fight with the VPD over juris-diction too."

I stepped back into the hall as the car drove away. "I'm not sure I want to work with you anymore."

26

My anger hadn't waned by the time we got to my place. David followed me through the security gate and down the finger dock. He didn't say anything. I guess he'd become used to holding things in until we were inside to avoid the neighbors.

I stole a glance at him as I unlocked the door; he didn't look angry. I punched in the alarm code and went to the kitchen. Wine. It might not calm me, but it would help me get through the conversation I knew was coming. David not being mad wasn't a great situation because I didn't know him enough to guess how good he was at hiding his feelings. If he was angry, it meant Andy did the right thing in his eyes. That was bad.

"Hungry?" he asked. "I can order pizza."

"I had a big lunch, but you go ahead if you need to eat." I took two glasses to the kitchen table and poured while he called the local pizza place.

It didn't take long; the restaurant knew what I liked, and David's phone was linked to my information now. He confirmed the usual order and hung up.

"I need to know where Nora is," I said. "Glenda will want to be sure she's okay."

"I can find that for you," he said. He took a sip from his glass. "Good wine."

He wasn't going to start the conversation. There was no way he didn't realize we'd be having one, but it was up to me. The thing is, I didn't want to provoke him, and I couldn't think how to begin without doing so.

"When are you heading to the hospital?" he asked.

"She's in surgery and won't be out for a few hours. I'll go tomorrow when she'll probably be in a ward."

Maybe I was stalling because the pizza delivery would interrupt whatever happened when I asked the first question.

"Okay, I'll make sure Andy authorizes you to visit. Someone will be guarding her while she's in recovery."

I'd forgotten that I needed permission. "If he doesn't let me see her, I'll find a way."

"What? Dress up as a nurse and sneak in?" He laughed.

"If I must. This isn't funny. It's my job to make sure nothing more goes wrong."

He didn't respond. All he had to say was my job was over. Then I could tell him what I thought of Andy and his boss. I might need to deal with them to talk to my client, but no one could force me to work with them.

"What did Andy say to you before we left?" he asked.

Didn't he hear? Or was he prompting me to think?

The security door buzzer announced the delivery guy. "I'll meet him up there. Be back in a second," David said.

I was alone and thinking about what Andy told me. He would get me back on the case. If he was sincere, I would have no trouble seeing Glenda tomorrow. But did I want back in?

David returned and placed the box on the table. He grabbed two plates and then took the first slice.

"I said I wasn't hungry." The pizza did smell delicious. "Andy told me to back off. That he wanted me back on the investigation but I would have to let him deal with it."

"It won't take long. Michel needed someone to vent on and he chose you."

"So, he'll go meekly into the background and Andy is about to call and invite me back after telling me I blew the case?" Some of my anger receded as we talked, leaving room for me to feel hungry. I grabbed a slice and waited.

"He was out of line. They both were. No one blew the case alone. You did your part. You told him it was a bad idea. But Andy didn't expect Alan to slip the observers and come home. And we don't know if he came back because he was suspicious."

"But I took all the blame," I said. "I can't keep fighting him. He doesn't listen to me. He'll get someone killed, and I won't be part of that."

David took another slice of pizza and looked at me as he chewed. I was missing something, but he didn't plan on making it easy on me by telling me. I picked the mushrooms off my slice and ate them. My stomach, confused between hunger and stress, left me feeling a little nauseated between bites. "You think I should work with them if he asks."

"I think you bring baggage to the relationship that gets in the way. You think he doesn't care about civilians. You think he's using you. Then something happens to reinforce that feeling and you can't see all the times he helped or supported you."

"Beyond having an RCMP big shot yelling at me after they caused my client to be beaten within an inch of her life?" I pushed the plate away and grabbed my glass. "The bigger picture? Yeah, hard to see around the blood and broken bones."

He stopped eating and poured more wine into both glasses. "If Alan hadn't come home unexpectedly, he'd have a bug in the house. Glenda would be safe, and Nora would be home. I'm pretty sure our presence tipped him over the edge, but he didn't come home because we were there."

"The people watching him were RCMP," I said in a final effort to assign blame so I could let myself off the hook. "They lost him; they didn't let Andy know right away. If they'd sent a text, we would have left. Glenda would be safe, and Nora would be home."

"And someone will be getting shit for that. But what happened was inevitable. Blackhouse is a violent man involved with a dangerous crowd. You know from your investigations that you can't control every detail."

I wasn't mad any longer, just tired. "I can't trust him. Yeah, yeah, my baggage, but I can't let Andy stop me from finding Alan so he can be sent to jail for what he did."

"And if Andy gives you that chance? If he brings you into the bigger investigation?"

"If he asks, I'll talk to him," I said. "I'm not waiting for him to reach out. I'm not promising I'll agree to help him. I will listen."

"All I can ask," David said. "Remember, you don't officially have a case any longer. You proved Alan was up to something, so your job is done."

"We'll see what Glenda has to say about that," I said. "I'm going to bed. Are you joining me?"

He closed the box, put the pizza in the fridge and brought the wine upstairs.

27

I t was hard to get up and out of the house without waking David. Andy hadn't called, and so I felt no obligation to sit on the sidelines until he asked me to play. It was only five a.m. so no point in calling the hospital about Glenda. There were plenty of things I could do, and not all of them made me feel like I was hiding something from David.

Of course, I wasn't going to do any of the innocent things.

It's not like I was doing anything wrong. Just going to talk to someone. No dangerous forays into Kuznetsov's territory. Only a little dip into the Hells Angels pool. Guy knew more than he told me, and I was not going to let that continue.

Most of his buddies would be sleeping the previous night off. If I could get him to meet me, we should be able to keep it a secret.

On the off chance he couldn't make a meet, I didn't go far; to the security gate, not through to the street. I called his number and waited. It went to voicemail. No room to leave a message even if I wanted to do so. I figured he'd filled the box with his own calls to disable the service.

He'd see who reached out. I think he listed me in his contacts as Cherry. I guess he didn't have an actual Cherry in his life. Unless he was asleep, he'd call back soon — I hoped.

Standing at the security gate felt weird. No one was around, but that wouldn't last. People in the buildings across the way would be out soon walking their dogs or getting in their morning run. Someone would notice me and think I was lurking.

I slipped through and headed to the nearest Starbucks. Two minutes later my phone buzzed with a text. I couldn't persuade Guy by text, but it wasn't him anyway. David.

Where u go?

Walking. Not exactly a lie.

Off to work. With a heart emoji.

Heart emoji. *See you later.*

Off the hook. Good, I preferred doing my job without worrying about David's approval. And I know he didn't expect to give me approval; that was a version of my baggage. I would work on that when I had time.

By the time Guy called, I had my latte and muffin in hand and was headed for a bench in the park.

"I'm busy, Charity, what do you want now?"

"Good morning to you, Guy. Sorry. Rough night."

"I'm working and haven't been to bed yet. What do you want?"

I didn't ask what he was working on. Whatever kept a Hells Angels biker up all night wasn't my business. And I had no desire to make it my business.

"I need some more information on Blackhouse, or his boss."

I got the answer I expected. "No."

"Okay, here's the deal." I told him about Glenda, leaving out the RCMP involvement, not because I wanted to protect Andy, but because I worried I'd lose Guy as a contact if I brought all kinds of federal weight to the table. "I need to figure this out so Nora can go back to her mom."

"Isn't the kid being taken care of by a foster home?"

"You think that's a good result?"

He was stalling. He knew that a foster situation was as likely to be bad as good. And for a kid who saw her mother beaten so badly by her dad?

"Emotional blackmail is unfair," he said.

"Really? Fairness matters to a gang member?" I made the words light. Guy and I had a weird relationship. I could tease until he decided I couldn't. Since I rarely received warning that I was pushing too hard, I couldn't do anything to avoid it. I trusted Guy not to come punish me over anything, let alone a gentle poke at his ethics.

"Fine. I can meet you at the same place as last time. I won't have long. I'm with people right now."

"Half an hour?"

"Be there." He ended the call and I ran to pick up my car.

ON THE DRIVE OVER, I remembered the last encounter. I'd come close to being caught. Then I was disguised as a hooker. I didn't think of that when I got dressed. Tee shirt, jeans, hoodie didn't come across as easy to remove like a pro would wear. That left me with having to come across as a junkie. In my experience, not as simple as it seems.

David might be useful if he knew what I was doing, but he might also show up with a few of his uniformed buddies.

That would scare off Guy, and maybe get him a beat down from his fellow gang members.

It was easier when I didn't have a man in my life who carried a gun and a badge. Without the possibility of getting one legally, I didn't even think of asking for a weapon, and I knew too much about street guns to take a chance with one of those. The last time I had the authorities on my side resulted in Glenda being almost killed. I didn't call David. I would rely on my wit and skill, and an enormous amount of luck. And Guy. He'd make sure I didn't get murdered, or gang raped. I'm pretty sure he would anyway.

I parked the car ten minutes early for our appointment. Arriving in the alley before he expected me was not smart. I had no idea what excuse he'd use to get away. I used the time to make myself look a little less clean and law abiding. I teased my hair into a mess and found some dirt in a gutter to rub into my jeans and leave on my hands. Then I checked to make sure I had a lot of wipes in my trunk to clean the evidence off as soon as I got back.

Guy had information for me. He wouldn't have agreed to meet otherwise. He will help. I'll be back in my car unhurt in less than twenty minutes. It was like a mantra as I walked the few blocks to the alley. If I kept repeating the words, maybe whoever ran the universe would listen and agree.

The street was empty, so no witness, reliable or not, to me entering the alley. Good because no one would follow. Bad because no one would hear me scream if things went sideways.

28

I picked my way down the alley. This time in the morning, the more fragrant aspects were fresh, and I wanted to back out to take a lungful of clean air. Since that was only a temporary fix, I just breathed shallowly and kept going. This time Guy turned the corner as I made it to the meeting point. He was down the same alley as before, not a surprise, but how many times can you beat up someone who owes you money?

"You should leave this alone," he said. "I don't like helping you get into trouble. You did me a favor and I owe you, but getting you killed doesn't seem to be the right payback."

He was very chatty today. Maybe working through the night broke down his reticence. Or maybe he was high. I tried not to look for evidence. It wasn't my job to tell him to be careful. He'd made his choices. I wouldn't stand by and let him distribute drugs in front of me, or abuse women, but I didn't let myself think too much about any of his activities.

"It won't take long," I said. "I need to get to the hospital and then go visit a little girl who doesn't know if her mom is alive or dead."

"Maybe she's better off with professionals."

If only that could be true. "She's already gone through the adoption process once. She needs stability."

"Fine, it's your life. I don't have a lot of detail. We try not to get too close to the Russians, but they are persistent. I avoid being around them, period."

Smart choice. I didn't want Guy hurt either. He might be a dangerous gang member, but he cared about his family, and he always tried to make me safe before giving me what I wanted. "I can follow up on anything."

"Your boyfriend helping?"

"No more than I need," I said. "He's a cop and has to stay within the rules. I don't. I get results faster."

He glanced back to the turn in the alley, to where he'd been before I arrived. "They bought the kid, right?"

"I don't think Glenda knew. Alan did all the work to adopt Nora and left her upbringing to Glenda."

"You ever met the guy who runs the place?" He looked back again then leaned against the fence, indicating I should do the same.

The fence was gross, but I'd be hidden to anyone coming to find Guy. So, I gritted my teeth, said a farewell to my favorite jacket and followed his advice.

"No. I met the secretary, but he was out. I saw his photo on the brochure and website." I hadn't been able to tie him to any crimes beyond the adoptions.

"The picture is faked. It's someone who looks a bit like him, but different enough to raise a little reasonable doubt. The receptionist is his wife. She keeps up the pretense of legitimate business."

No wonder I couldn't find him anywhere online. A

search of the image on the website led to a few articles, but nothing useful. "Whose picture is it?"

"Some dead sucker. Well, he was alive when they took the photo. Aren't you interested in what this Viktor guy looks like?"

"Just tell me." My gut was giving me signals that had nothing to do with the bodily fluids and not so fluid things permeating my nose. This was going to lead somewhere. "We're in a hurry, right?"

"Like the picture, a redhead, but not the same shade. He's harder looking too. I don't know who he is exactly to the gang. I know the Russian spelling of Viktor is a K, not a C. And I know he's not only selling kids for adoption."

"Are the police involved?" David would have told me, but I'm not sure I shared what I'd learned about Nora's origins. And I didn't need the RCMP to find my clues, thank goodness.

"Not helping as far as I can tell. He's on the DL right now, but your buddy Alan knows everything, I'm sure. The money guy learns way more than is safe in these situations."

"I think the money guy doesn't always realize how deep they are. Until they get arrested."

"Or end up on the wrong side of two in the back of the head." Guy pulled out a cigarette. "You need to figure out who else your man is hanging out with. I don't think Ivan is worried. At least there's no buzz about a change, and we usually get a heads up. Their money guy manages the trans-actions we do with the mob too."

Only a matter of time. "Am I a bitch for thinking it would be better for my client and her daughter if Alan was dead?"

Guy chuckled. "As long as Ivan doesn't think they need to be taken out too. You never know with these guys. But I'm guessing Alan convinced his boss that the wife was in the dark. Or she wouldn't have survived the beating I'm guessing Ivan ordered. You don't know if the husband is still alive either, right?"

"Why do people like him get involved in this stuff? They have good jobs. They are respected for what they do. Black-house had a family that loved him." Not everyone who goes into the law is a crooked cop or a mob lawyer. Not every person in finance is a money launderer. Not every surgeon is sewing up bullet holes on the side. But something attracts people with choices to this life.

"Drugs. Money problems, maybe a little addiction to kinky sex. And some people like the danger and power they think comes with the life." He took a drag and looked up like he was thinking about his past. "No one keeps the power for long. Eventually someone worse comes along. People are killed and the power passes on."

"And some of them get caught."

"That doesn't mean as much as you think, Charity."

"How deep do you think Alan might be?" If he could cut a deal, Glenda had no leverage. I needed to make sure she was ready to run if things came to that.

"Guy. Stop pissing around." The words preceded a big man around the corner. His jacket was covered in patches announcing his status in the gang. His face ruddy where it wasn't swallowed by the bush of a gray beard.

I would not make it to the street before he reached me.

"Just go with it," Guy said as he turned slowly to face the giant. "A cigarette and a happy ending."

29

I wiped my nose and looked down at the ground. I'd seen enough women driven to alley blow jobs for a fix to be able to mimic their behavior. What I didn't know was where we were supposed to be in that scenario. Had I done the deed?

"Stick," Guy said. "Just go back. I've got this. I'll be there in five."

Stick didn't listen. He walked toward me, radiating menace. I took a step back; the street was not that far if I could get a big enough lead. He was a giant and his belly might slow him down, but he had stride. I'd be taking three steps to his one. Great time for my luck to find another beneficiary.

"We're done. The cops won't find anything. I got five minutes." He joined us and now I was within arm's reach.

"I got a place to be," I said. "Thanks for the stuff. See you around."

"Maybe find another sucker," Guy said. "I get better service from my girlfriend, and she bathes regularly."

Keep your mouth shut. This situation is where I should let the men speak. But if Guy dumped me, it made me fair game for Stick. "You used to like what I do."

"I got needs," Stick said. "And like I said, I got time." The glare I got from Guy was almost enough to drop me. He wanted me to go, and I kept screwing things up. Well, he wasn't scared shitless, and he wasn't in danger of rape.

"Yeah, well find it somewhere else," I said. "You're not my type."

He cocked his head and gave me a slow smile, licking his lips like it was sexy. "I got more stuff than Guy. The good shit." His right hand went to his zipper, his left hand grabbed my arm.

"Stick, let her go. Man, she is bat-shit crazy. It's not worth it."

"Worth it for you," Stick said. "What's going on? You trying to keep her to yourself? If she's trouble, why's she still walking around?"

I shifted my weight to my toes. I would run, but if I tried now, I'd drop Guy in a pile of shit. I wish I'd told David where I was. At least he would find my body before it started to decompose.

"Old girlfriend," Guy said. He took a step in my direction. "I didn't notice the crazy to start with. Then she got hooked, you know how that goes."

"She clean?" Stick asked, still focused on his happy ending.

"Not a clue. But disease isn't the problem. She's a stalker. And she sticks like dog shit. And she's got too many friends to get away with stopping her with a bullet."

I pulled to free my arm, but Stick was too strong. "Let me go now, or I start screaming. I bring the cops here and you are fucked."

"No one to hear you," Stick said.

Someone's phone buzzed. Not mine.

"Let me go and you'll never see me again," I said. If the words shook, it only helped sell the role. I knew it was fear. Stick might mistake the emotion for anger. "I'll forget seeing you. I'll move. Go to Montreal. Just let me go." I punctuated the last words with tugs to free my arm with no effect.

A different phone buzzed. Someone really wanted to get hold of these two.

Guy pulled out his phone and checked. "We're out of time." He grabbed Stick's arm. "The boss just got the heads up. Cops are on the way. We need to be someplace else right now."

Stick still didn't let go. At some point, Guy was going to have to leave me to my fate or do something drastic that would put himself in danger. I wasn't sure his gratitude for the favor I did him extended to risking his life for me.

"Yeah, you gotta run," I said. Well, a junkie wouldn't be smart enough to give up the opportunity to lash out. "Your boss is calling. Hurry home to mommy."

The pressure on my arm increased to the point I thought the bone would snap. Stick let me go before it did. I wasn't going to be able to hide this bruise from David. But I had time to think up a story. Or find a way to tell the truth without making the situation sound so dire he locked me up for my own safety.

"I see you around again, I take what I want." Stick turned away from glaring at me to spit on the ground before saying to Guy, "You disappear again like that, and the boss and that Russian prick will know about it."

Guy glared at me again and then turned away.

His look kept my response inside my head. Stick probably wouldn't react well to being called a baby again.

They didn't even turn to check where I was. A good

thing because now that I was free to leave, I couldn't make my feet move.

They turned the corner, and I was alone. I took in a deep breath, regretting it immediately when I got a lungful of urine and vomit-flavored air. But the stench did kick me out of the paralysis. My legs were too shaky to run, but I managed to walk out to the street. Only six-thirty in the morning, but the sun was up, and the world seemed safer now that I was outside the alley.

I breathed again and my lungs filled with the city version of fresh air, gas fumes, and only a little urine. I was alive. No one had raped me. I hadn't had to fight off a biker the size of a mountain. Guy was safe. I had a few scraps of information. I would focus on those things, not on the might-have-beens. I couldn't even convince myself that I would never be in that position again.

I got back to my car and slid inside, pulled out a handful of wipes and scrubbed the filth off my skin and jacket. I might not smell clean, but wipe aroma was better than eau de alley. I gathered up the mess and found a garbage can a block away.

My phone buzzed as I walked back to the car. Guy calling to tell me to get lost? I looked at the screen. David, inviting me to breakfast.

30

I love breakfast in a restaurant. All the bacon and eggs and none of the cleanup. David was waiting for me when I arrived at the White Spot downtown. The location sat more or less halfway between us when he messaged me, far enough for me to get myself together, but not so far that David would ask questions.

"You left the house early," he said when the waitress walked away to place our order.

The same woman who served me and Andy. I was becoming a regular and I couldn't tell how I felt about it.

"I had something to follow up on." I unwrapped my cutlery to avoid looking at him. Not a lie, but if I met his eyes, I might disclose more than I planned. If he knew how close I'd come to... nope. I'm not going to think about it. I had a lead on Viktor and confirmation the Angels were linked to Ivan, so the risk panned out, and nothing happened.

"On the Blackhouse case?"

He knew I didn't have another active one.

"Yes, maybe someone who might know where Alan is hiding out."

"You'll tell Andy?" There was less of a question and more of an order in his voice.

I stopped fussing with the knife and fork and picked through the packs of jam. "If he asks."

"You should use him," David said. "I know how you feel. I agree, he screwed up. But you need protection, or support."

"I don't," I said and made the mistake of looking at him. He was frowning but his anger wasn't directed at me. "What? Is there something on my face?"

"What happened this morning?"

I shouldn't have taken my attention away from the jams. Where was our food? Why didn't the waitress interrupt us? "I met with a contact. He gave me some information."

"No. You look like you've been to the edge of something bad." He waited for me to speak.

I tried to sort my thoughts into some kind of order. Just blurting out the events wouldn't end well. I needed to control the flow so David would still listen after the Stick part of the story. I gave up and said, "I'm fine. Nothing happened."

Now our food arrived, and I could waste more time in adding sauce, salt, and pepper. Not a lot of time, and David didn't plan to let it go. He watched me as I tried to find another activity to avoid talking.

Nothing, and I reminded myself I wasn't a five-year-old. An adult dealt with things head on.

"I'm not telling you who my contact is," I said. "But he's not exactly law-abiding. No good resource is, right?"

He agreed with me and then picked up his breakfast sandwich.

"So, he didn't have a name, but he told me to look at the

adoption guy. He's not who he claims to be." My eggs were getting cold, so I slid them on a slice of toast to capture the yolk and cut off a mouthful.

"And this is why your face is white as a sheet?" He started on his hash browns.

Now that I had to say the words, my appetite slipped away. The eggs looked deflated and sickly, and the bacon smelled like hot lumps of fatty salt. "There was a bit of a problem when I went to leave."

"If you don't tell me what's going on, I can't support you," he said.

"I couldn't bring you along, because he wouldn't show up. He knows about you, and it already changed the dynamic."

"I wasn't suggesting you needed a police escort." He pushed his plate away; maybe his taste buds were in rebellion too. "We could have set up something to keep you safe without blowing it for you."

Like having a cruiser pull up if I gave some mysterious signal? "Anything you did might have fooled the guy who threatened me, but I'd lose my contact and I can't afford to do that. He helps me on cases that don't involve the Russian Mob. I'm fine. Nothing happened. We handled the situation."

"What's your next move?"

His question confused me. What happened to the argument I anticipated only a second ago?

He hadn't actually said he'd back off, but the subject change was more than a sidestep. "Follow up on the information I found." I picked up a slice of bacon. The aroma was back, reminding me I hadn't eaten for a long while. "I guess I'll go by the hospital first. See if Glenda is awake."

"What's the information?" I must have glared at him

because he laughed. Not the reaction I wanted from a supportive boyfriend. "I'm not going to stop you. I can't help if I don't understand what you need."

I didn't believe him. Not because he was a cop, but because I was going to be in jeopardy and he wanted me safe. The minute I started to investigate Viktor, alarms would go off. And not just in Ivan's world. Andy would find out I was digging into his case. David might think he would let me do what I wanted, but... I guess the only way to find out was to tell him.

"The guy who runs the adoption agency. I didn't meet him. I saw his picture on brochures and on their website, but it's a fake. His name is probably a cover too. I need to track down the real Viktor and find out how he's connected."

His face tightened and he didn't answer right away. I gave him credit for not immediately saying it was too dangerous, but I figured that argument was going on in his head.

"If you don't know what he looks like, or his name, or anything really, where will you start?"

Okay, that sounded like he decided to help. "Well, apparently he does kind of look like the picture. And I'll be going through Alan's financial records. The payment for Nora must be somewhere."

"Any other approaches you can't tell me about?" He was smiling again. "I know you don't stick with the usual legal tools. No PI can do their job without some shady help."

The answer was yes, of course I had access to methods I couldn't tell him about. I could track Alan's phone log and try to find Viktor's number, then track him. Everything up to the last thing stayed within the rules because Glenda agreed to my investigation. Once I got to Viktor, the important part, I was more than shady.

"I have all kinds of tools," I said. "I'm pretty sure you shouldn't get involved."

He looked over my shoulder and nodded at someone. I turned, ready to defend my actions if it turned out to be Andy. It was our waitress.

David paid the bill, and we left the restaurant. As soon as I stepped through to the street my phone buzzed. This time it was Andy.

31

I slid to ignore. I didn't have the strength or patience to deal with him now. David looked at the screen but didn't comment. Smart man.

"I'm going to the hospital." I kissed his cheek and turned away.

My phone buzzed again. Andy. I ignored the call again.

"He won't give up," David said. "Better if you just get it over with."

What I wanted to do was block the number, but he had access to a lot of different phone lines. Law enforcement is hard to dodge even if you are legitimate.

"Stick around," I said. "I might need you to protect him."

David chuckled and nodded to his car. "Probably not a good idea to do this on the street then."

By the time he called again, we were sitting in the car. "What?"

"Good morning," he said.

I put the phone on speaker. "I'm busy, what do you want?"

"Nothing. I figured you wanted an update."

"Yes." I didn't believe it would come without conditions, but whatever he gave would save me time. "Go ahead."

"First, your client is out of surgery. She's in pretty bad shape but will fully recover."

"Thanks. I'm visiting her today."

"I'll let the officer on guard know. But she's being kept under to allow her body to heal."

At least they were protecting her, and I wouldn't waste the time it took to go to the hospital to find out she wasn't awake. "Will I get a call when she's ready?"

"Yes. Unless she doesn't want to see you. I think the best thing is for you to send your bill to the house and walk away now," he said.

David pressed mute on the phone, and I glared at him.

"Don't just say no," David said. "If you can't make a working deal, he can arrest you for interfering with an ongoing investigation."

I hit the mute button again. "I still have some loose ends. I'm not going to run away from this. As long as I have a contract, I have a job. So, until my client says otherwise, I'm still looking into what trouble her husband is in." Maybe I managed to inject a little professional concern past the stubbornness, but I truly didn't care. David didn't say anything or stop me continuing the call.

"The daughter, Nora, is settled with the foster parents. No one is in danger; your job is done."

What happened to the offer to work together? Had his boss, Michel, convinced him to cut ties?

"You aren't my client. I'm not breaking any laws. I'm not getting in your way." *At least right now when I'm sitting in a cop's car.* "Thank you for the update. How is your case going?"

David grunted and I noticed his eyes roll. He wasn't angry, so one less wall to kick down.

"We continue to follow leads," Andy said. "Your job, however, is complete. Your client has all the information she needs to decide on her next steps. We'll be requesting her cooperation when she is conscious. She has every incentive to take our protection and end her association with you."

I guess that meant I wouldn't get any real updates. And I wondered if Glenda was really unconscious. Perhaps it was a lie to keep me from talking to her. Unfortunately, Andy had way more to offer her than I did. He could put her in a version of witness protection. He could stop Child Protection from taking Nora away. He probably had a heap of evidence to convince her that Alan was a real criminal. All I had was a client relationship. If Andy got to Glenda first, I'd take the blame for yesterday, and I'd be lucky to get paid. And I was the only one making progress on the case.

I did know a lot more about Glenda than Andy did, though. The official investigation hadn't touched her more than a quick dismissal. And she wouldn't be much help in getting a conviction. There was no point asking her permission to bug the house if Alan was unlikely to return. And he had gone into hiding, so there was no tearful apology and promise to never do that again in Glenda's future so they could grab him.

"Why the change of heart? You wanted me working with you; you told me to wait yesterday." I was not going to stop investigating, but knowing the reason I was no longer wanted might be useful.

"My boss doesn't think it's a good idea to bring in civilians. And this is too dangerous for you to go further. Putting you in can complicate the prosecution."

Those were not his reasons. He was following orders. I

couldn't be sure if he wanted my help, or that he'd follow through on the threat to arrest me for interfering. I wasn't stepping back. Alan knew who I was, and he would tell Ivan if he had any hint it would save him. And I didn't want RCMP protection. I had a life, and David would be forced to drop a career he loved. I'd dealt with criminals before.

"If I find anything out, I'll pass it on," I said. David wasn't looking at me any longer. He stared out the side window at the street.

"If you get in our way, I'll stop you," Andy said. "This is serious, Charity. Forget that these guys will kill you to avoid even the hint of a risk of getting caught. They are powerful. If we don't pull them in fast, they will be entrenched, and more people will die."

"And you haven't made a lot of headway," I said. "Are you trying to tell me they've already infiltrated your organization?" Was Michel on their payroll? Was I supposed to be reading between the lines here? Not one of my strengths.

"I'm telling you to step back," Andy said. "If I had proof of any corruption, I'd know how to report it."

"I appreciate the warning." I stared out of the windshield and past the dead bugs. The street was filling now that people were heading into work. David was still behaving like he wasn't part of the conversation. No bolt of lightning or ray of sunshine to point the way to the right choice. I took that to mean, be yourself.

"Charity, I know you are still there," Andy said. "I need an answer."

He wouldn't like my decision, and I didn't want to keep talking about this in case I told him too much about what I learned this morning. "I hear your warnings. Inform me when Glenda wakes up, please."

I ended the call and turned to David. "Thanks for the help."

He shook his head at me, but no frown. "You did fine. And you don't want me to tell you to be safe. I trust you, and I will be there to help."

32

"You didn't say much." Now that I was free to go, I didn't relish the idea of sitting around thinking. Despite all my resistance to stepping off and leaving things to the professionals, I had nothing immediate to do. Yes, research on Viktor, but spending the day in front of my computer searching for his identity didn't sound exciting enough. I guess that's how adrenaline junkies start out. I was crashing from the excitement of a few hours ago and wanting a fix.

"You did fine," he said, again. "Where's your car?"

"You don't want me working on this case, right?" I asked without thinking.

He sighed and turned to me. "Why are you trying to provoke a fight?"

"I'm not." Okay, I was, and I knew it came from stress; I'm not that self-unaware. Being keyed up wasn't only from Stick's lovely threats; the whole situation piled up with emotions. Guilt over Glenda and Nora, frustration that no single clue let me move toward a resolution. A sneaking suspicion no one could get Ivan off the streets, and even if they did, someone else waited in the wings. And not a better citizen. Life didn't work that way.

The world would continue to spin, the universe would bend to justice the way Martin Luther King promised, but not to individual justice. And none of it was David's fault.

"What can I do?" David asked. "I said I'm here to help, but I don't know how you want me to assist."

"I'm not being fair," I said. "I'm sorry. I'm having a shitty week and there's no sign of an end."

"I can talk to Andy about bringing you back in. I'm pretty sure he's acting under some pressure from above."

If he reacted like this, I couldn't afford to align myself with the investigation. I'd be fighting to keep working every time I took action. I'm terrible at taking time to think things through, let alone asking for permission before jumping in with both eyes closed.

I said all this to David. "And he won't be happy with me either. He's right, I might screw the long-term goal up."

David stared out the windshield again. The scene hadn't changed much. It was brighter, but that just highlighted the gray of the concrete buildings. More people on the sidewalk, more bikes and cars on the road as people started their day.

He didn't speak for a bit. The light on the corner turned red, then green and then back to red before he turned to face me. "If he agrees to your terms, will you try?"

His voice was hopeful, and I hated to break it to him that the odds were very long on that happening.

"I'm not going to slam the door in his face," I said. "And maybe he has information I need. Ways to find Viktor's real identity, to track Alan down. But he's not asking, or he's taking too long to ask. I can't sit around doing nothing." I realized I hadn't listed how I would help Andy, but I didn't think my preferences would be part of the deal. He wanted to use me and order me around.

"You should have told Andy about that," he said. "The Viktor thing."

See, there's the difference between being a cop and being a private investigator. David's first, second, and third thought was about involving the authorities. My every thought focused on doing my job by myself so no one could screw anything up. No one other than me, anyway.

"Do you think I had the opportunity? He didn't want to hear anything I said."

"I'm not going to argue about it," David said. "It's up to him to reach out. I'm not asking you to call him."

Did that mean he wouldn't tell Andy about Viktor? "Must you tell him about my lead?"

"No. I don't have a legal requirement to load him up with every rumor about his case. If he asks, I'm not going to lie. If you disappear, I'm calling him first," David said. "I will be reprimanded if he finds out, but I get shit all the time."

"Thanks." I believed him. He wasn't going to narc on me. I was safe to continue with my job. "There is one thing."

He opened the window and put his police light on the roof of the car. "I can't park here much longer," he said. "What do you need?"

"Nora. When I talk to Glenda, I want to be able to tell her Nora is doing okay. Can you find out where she's staying?"

"Yes. But you need to be careful. They won't let just anyone visit. And if you lie about who you are, they'll contact the cops."

It was going to get in my way, but I couldn't blame them. "Does that apply to Alan? Will they let her dad drop by after almost killing her mother?"

"No," David said. He started the car. "I'm the contact. He's on a list of risks. If he shows up, they call 911. I meant when you go there, don't pull any investigative tricks. I won't be able to fix it if CPS decides you are a danger to the kid."

"Where is she?"

"I need to check who took her in. I'll call you."

"You are a hero," I said and leaned over to kiss his cheek.

"Yes, I am," he said. "Can I drop you at your car?"

I opened my door. "I'm not far. I promise to make it there without causing any problems."

He laughed and pulled away from the curb as soon as I shut the door.

So, my day was going to be boring. I guess if you start with a threat in an alley in a bad part of town, a quiet afternoon of research should be welcome.

I picked up a few groceries on my way home so I wouldn't have to stop working to make lunch. I got in the door and the smell of cleaner hit me when I took off my jacket. I needed a shower and clean clothes. I put the coffee pot on to brew and ran upstairs.

I had the address and contact details for Nora's foster parents before I finished my first mug of coffee. I glanced at my computer, then the clock. Still a bit early to call about the kid. I sat and started poking around the internet for some way to find the real Viktor.

33

I called the foster family and got voicemail. I left a message with my phone number and then decided I had nothing better to do than research Viktor. It wasn't going to be as easy as stalking his social media, but it was hard to hide yourself completely. Knowing his receptionist was his wife would be a starting point. Cynthia something would help me solve this case.

The website didn't contain much information, but if they wanted it to look legit to the authorities, she might be on payroll. That meant some kind of audit requirements, and even if it went to another cover business, it would give me something. At the bottom of the home page, I found a link to *Our Company*. And it became that easy: a law firm, an accountant, and a list of major suppliers.

If Andy didn't have this information, it gave me some leverage next time he put pressure on me. I ignored the accountant and lawyer in favor of the name listed as Community Liaison: Cynthia Towers.

My phone rang just as I started a series of searches for

Mrs. Towers. The call display showed the foster home. "Charity Deacon," I said.

"Ms. Deacon, this is Prem Gupta. You called about one of the children?"

I liked that she was cagey about the name. Nora needed protecting and that meant it shouldn't be easy to get to her. "Yes. I'd like to see her if it's okay. Her mother will confirm she knows me." Shit, Glenda was unconscious. I didn't want to ask Andy to give permission, but I guess I didn't have a choice.

"We are going to visit her mother a little later," Prem said.

So, no one thought to call me when Glenda woke up. At least my slip up wouldn't stop me seeing Nora at some point. I figured if I knew she'd come out of the anesthetic, I might sound like a good guy. "I'll be doing the same thing," I said. "When are you planning to be there?"

"I don't know our schedule," Prem said. "I'm sure we don't need to worry about how many people visit at once."

Weird, normal visiting rules restricted the number of visitors, and with the cops protecting her, I'm sure Glenda's restrictions would be tighter. "I'll head down now. That way Glenda will know you are coming. She'll tell you I have permission to visit her daughter when you get there. After you've talked to Glenda, tell me when I can come by. I'm sure Nora will be happy to see a familiar face."

She said nothing. Was I supposed to explain why I knew that? Had I said the wrong thing?

"Sorry," Prem said. "I had to deal with a little tantrum. Yes. The child is feeling the effects of the trauma. If you can give her some assurance, it will help. I will reach out to you as soon as I confirm your identity and that you are not out to harm the girl."

The call left me with a stew of mixed feelings. Nora needed protection, and I needed to make sure she was in a safe home so Glenda could relax and heal. But Prem's cold and professional attitude made me question if she could fill a nurturing role. Was that the right approach? Or perhaps she just used it for me, a stranger? I had no idea what Nora knew about her father. I couldn't even be sure if she saw Alan beat her mother, or just came down to the aftermath.

I also didn't know what being separated from her mother would do to her as an adopted child. I sat trying to work out what I should be doing long enough for my coffee to go cold and my computer to go to sleep.

I dumped the coffee and made another cup. I hit a key on the laptop to wake the system and then focused on the screen. There were a bunch of hits on Cynthia Towers, one or two images with her husband. He was the same guy as on the website and brochure. Since he was dead, the photos were old. I put aside my concerns about Nora. She was with the people who had the skills to care for her, and I wasn't one of them. Finding Viktor and linking him to Alan and Ivan was my job. That would make her safe for the future.

I set a timer for a half hour to let me dig deep into the links and still leave me time to go to the hospital before lunch.

I opened a new tab and searched for Viktor Towers. The results were pretty much the same as on the Cynthia search. I clicked on a few of the links, and then bookmarked the interesting results so I could check back easily. I didn't find a major revelation. Cynthia and Viktor Towers were active in their community, members of the right social clubs. They played tennis and ate in decent restaurants. But all of that was fairly new activity.

Neither Viktor nor Cynthia appeared on social media three years ago.

No tagging on their or other people's posts. They didn't like any of the ubiquitous images or pithy sayings, instructions about loving yourself, or cute baby animals.

And none of the pictures I found were clear enough or of high enough resolution to pull an image search. If I didn't suspect them of current and ongoing criminal activity and associations, I'd swear they were in witness protection. Should I ask David to check? No. He wouldn't get an answer on that, and people who'd turned witness were supposed to keep a low profile and not run criminal businesses.

My alarm sounded and I had to stop looking for clues until I'd seen Glenda.

I changed clothes again. I was clean and I'd changed since, but I could smell the alley every time I moved. I stuck my laptop in my case, on the off chance I'd be hanging around waiting. I didn't have anything to follow up on after the hospital — unless Glenda remembered something. But I could do my online research in a coffee shop, rather than at my kitchen counter. Sometimes the bustle of the cafe prompted ideas that didn't come in the peace of the marina. And I needed a brilliant idea, or I would be forced to beg Andy for help and pay for it with my shred of information from Viktor's website.

Even the thought that I would be groveling made me feel sick.

34

I t wasn't as difficult as I expected to access Glenda's private room. Sean, the cop outside the open door, wore a VPD uniform. I wondered why Andy hadn't bothered to put an RCMP presence in the hall, but Sean was big enough to stop a couple of hitmen. If Alan sent anyone to finish the job, that is. Although, I guess it was possible that he thought Glenda died from the beating.

"Don't tire her out," the nurse said as she left the room with a vial of blood on a tray.

I'd forgotten how fond the nurses were of taking fluids for tests. When it was me in the bed, I didn't have the energy to care what they were doing. Now that I looked down at Glenda, I wanted to know everything. Was the test necessary? Were we sure the nurse was legit? Should Glenda have someone in the room instead of simply outside the door?

I dismissed the rush of questions as stress-induced paranoia. Her safety was in the hands of the professionals. My job was to get her husband off the streets so he couldn't do any more damage than he'd already done.

"Hi," I said, drawing up a chair.

She turned her head to me. Her body, held in place with all the needles and shunts and monitors, remained still. Glenda's eyes were dull. They had her on some strong painkillers and, until they decided she'd recovered enough to use a self-administered drip, they would keep her heavily doped.

"Nora is safe," I said. "You have a guard; did you know that?"

She licked her lips and then nodded.

Painkillers can leave you with a sticky mouth. I took the plastic glass of water and held the straw while she sipped. "Has anyone talked to you?"

"Andy." The word came out in a croak, and she nodded for more water.

"Is there someone you want me to call? It's no fun being here alone."

She shook her head. "Too dangerous." Her eyes drooped.

"The foster mom said she'll bring Nora around. Can you tell her I'm cleared to see her? I'm pretty sure I can get anything she needs from the house."

"Don't let Nora see me like this." The drowsiness was gone for the moment.

It was only temporary. The weight would come crashing back soon and take her unconscious mid-sentence, if I remembered the last time I was in the hospital correctly.

"She'll be better if she sees you are okay, because the last time she saw you shouldn't be the image she goes back to when she worries about you."

Glenda didn't respond.

"She needs to see you are alive," I said. "But you are her mom, and you can tell the cops or the doctor that you don't want her to come."

She still didn't speak, but a tear leaked out of each eye. I pulled a tissue from the little box on her bed table and dabbed at the moisture before it started burning her wounds.

"I'm still on the case," I said. "I will find Alan and make sure he's locked up. When you leave here, you and Nora will be safe."

"All this fuss isn't only about Alan, right?"

She'd rallied a bit, but her words carried a hopelessness that I wanted to hug away from her. None of my clients had ever brought out that feeling. Then again, none of my previous clients had been put in the hospital — it was usually me recovering from the beating.

Lying there depressed from her injuries and the meds, lonely and scared for her child and herself, Glenda showed nothing of the woman who hired me. How much more could she take? How much had Andy told her? And how much relief would she feel if she knew about Ivan?

If it was me, I hope I'd want the truth. Not knowing would set me agonizing over every idea that popped into my mind. The only thing in a hospital able to distract anyone from traveling down a rabbit hole of panic were meds. A bad crutch to lean on.

Her look made my decision for me. Through the fog of painkillers and recovery from surgery, she pleaded with me to tell her the truth. I knew that could be coming from something inside me. Once I started, I wouldn't be able to take anything back, so I asked first. "What do you know about the situation?"

"Alan is involved with dangerous people. I get witness protection if I talk. There must be more because I don't think I have any information worth protecting."

Her eyes closed, but as I settled back to wait for her to

come back to consciousness, she reached her hand toward me. I held it gently and started talking. "I don't know every-thing, but it's not just working in the gray area. They are looking at Alan for money laundering. His boss is a very dangerous man, and the RCMP will probably offer him a deal to turn on the boss."

"I don't know anything about it," she said.

"You do," I said, giving her hand a gentle squeeze. "You don't recognize it, but things you've told me are evidence. You just don't realize the importance. Trust the RCMP to figure everything out. They know what they are doing."

I patted her hand in comfort and waited. Glenda was trying to speak through the tears, and I had all the time in the world.

She finally managed to take control of her emotions. I gave her another sip of water and leaned in close, so she didn't have to strain to be heard.

"If I can't give them any information, will they still protect me and my child?"

I hadn't even thought of that problem. Would they? Protection cost money, and the budget was limited. I didn't know the answer, but Glenda didn't have the stamina to waste effort on that kind of fear. She needed her energy to heal, to look strong for her daughter, to help the cops.

"I know you have what they need," I said. "I'll find more for you. If they renege, I will make sure you are safe. I have resources, and you can use that money you salted away. Don't tell the RCMP about that and everything will be fine."

She stared at me. Trying to decide whether to believe me, I guess. I didn't blink, or smile, or try to say anything more.

Glenda nodded. "My phone help?"

"Yes, but your house is a crime scene."

"It was in my pocket. Look in the bag on the side table."

I pulled out a phone — dead, but I had the charger for it.

Glenda told me the code to unlock it, then blinked and didn't open her eyes again. Her hand let go of mine and I was grateful for the monitors that kept up a regular beeping, confirming she slept.

On my way out, I told the nurse that Glenda's daughter was coming, and if they could do anything to help her cover how bad her injuries looked, it would be kind.

35

I sat in my car for a few minutes before leaving, trying to push Glenda's injuries out of my mind. I didn't think anyone would be able to make her look well enough that her daughter wouldn't be scared. I couldn't do anything about that.

I'd promised to wait until the foster mom had gone to visit the hospital before checking on Nora, and now I regretted the decision. Good thing I had the address. If I showed up at the house, maybe I could talk to the kid first and prepare her for the sight of her mother. And I'd get to check if the home was good enough. No matter how much I told myself it was unusual for the wrong people to be made foster parents, every story of abuse and neglect shot into my brain.

And the cops had cleared me to visit, so they should let me in. The place was secure since it was under surveillance.

I started the car and headed toward Burnaby. The address was in a nice residential neighborhood I'd been on another case, so I didn't need the GPS.

Traffic was more than its usual crappy, slow crawl, and I

had to travel across the city. That meant three different rush hour flows along streets with lights every other intersection and no convenient shortcuts.

I pulled up outside a two-story house set on a street with trees too small to provide shade or buckle the sidewalk. More practical than Nora's old house. The yard was fenced with a small gate in front of a concrete path to the stairs. A few straggly roses occupied the corner, and the grass had its fair share of dandelions, but it didn't look neglected. Just a victim of bad soil, I guess.

I didn't hear any children playing or big dogs barking.

I headed to the door and rang the bell.

I was about to ring again as it opened. A short woman in a gray tee-shirt and jeans stood looking up at me.

She was probably in her forties and had that harried look I associated with women who had children. Her hair was tied back in a ponytail, and she didn't wear makeup. "Yes?"

"I called earlier," I said. "Charity Deacon."

"I said we'd contact you after seeing Nora's mother." She looked past me to the street.

Who did she think was there?

"I know, but the police must have told you I was safe," I said. "And I've just come from the hospital. Can I come in?"

Her eyes flicked back to the street, and I waited for her to say no. In her position, would I turn someone away? I kept a neutral smile on my face while she sorted out her decision.

Then she stood back and gestured for me to enter.

"I'm cleaning up after lunch," she said. "The kids are out in the backyard."

Now I could hear some playing noise. Not sweet trills of childish laughter, the shrieks children use to express everything from *I'm being murdered*, to *I'm having so much fun I'm about to explode.* I assumed if they meant the first, Mrs. Gupta wouldn't be inviting me into the kitchen.

She returned to loading the dishwasher. By the orange smears on the bowls, I guessed macaroni and cheese for lunch.

"Would you like some chai?" she asked. "It will only take a minute to heat some."

I liked the spices in chai, but I hated condensed milk. I could smell the slightly sweet, slightly off aroma. "I'm fine. I need to tell you about my visit."

She shrugged and turned the element up under a pan on the stove. "Suit yourself. Ms. Deacon, you can see I'm busy. Why are you here?"

"Call me Charity," I said. "As I said, Ms. Gupta, I just came from the hospital. I think it's a mistake to take Nora there without telling her how bad her mother looks."

She pulled a mug from the cupboard and gave a stir to the pan before replying. "You can call me Prem. I know her mother was beaten. I told Nora she shouldn't be scared."

I glanced out. Nora sat on the grass next to a wooden playhouse. Two boys and another girl were running around the perimeter of the yard in some complicated form of tag. Nora didn't even look at them.

"Glenda looks like she's about to die," I said. "Prem, it might be a good idea to wait a day."

My phone buzzed with an incoming text. I glanced down: David — later.

"She needs to be sure that her mother is alive." Prem poured a mug of chai and nodded to the table. "Have a seat and tell me exactly how bad it is."

"Before I do, how is she?" I cocked my head to the yard where Nora still sat alone.

"Nightmares all last night, poor thing. She is withdrawn.

We're hoping the other children will cheer her up, but they are kids, and if she doesn't want to play, they ignore her."

"And her father?"

"He's not allowed near," Prem said quickly. "If he tries to come in, we call 911. But I haven't noticed anyone hanging around."

There was supposed to be a protection detail. Of course, it was to their benefit to let Alan get close, so it made sense for them to be hidden. I told Prem what Glenda looked like. "I asked the nurse to try to clean her up a bit, but I'm not sure how much difference they can make."

My phone buzzed again. Another text from David. I put the phone on do not disturb.

"The last time she saw her mother..." Prem said.

"I know. Lying in a pool of blood." Maybe her current condition would look like an improvement. "Did she say anything? Nora? How much she saw or remembers?"

"She hasn't said much. Only please and thank you."

The back door opened, and Nora peeked inside.

As soon as she saw me, she ran and hugged me tight.

"I'll leave you to talk," Prem said. "I'll be in the office if you need me."

I pulled the kid onto my lap and gave her a hug back. "Do you want to visit your mom?"

She nodded. "Is she dead?"

I kissed the top of her head. "No, sweetie, but she has lots of owies."

She looked up at me and said, "I kiss them better."

I didn't get anything else from her, so I promised that she would visit her mother before I went to say goodbye to Prem.

She slapped her laptop closed as I leaned into the closet she called the office. I told her about our conversation.

"I'll take her soon as my husband gets home."

We said our goodbyes and I headed back to my car. I checked the street for surveillance. There was an SUV a half block away with tinted windows, and a utility van the same distance the other way.

I flipped on my phone and read the texts from David. *Call Andy. Where are you?*

I didn't want to start arguing again. Time to find Viktor or Alan, or anyone who could help me protect Glenda and Nora by putting them away.

36

I don't know what private investigators did in the days before free coffee shop wifi and power outlets. Sitting at home on my computer was my least favorite way to work a case. I hadn't found a more interesting way to research, but doing it with a latte from someone who knew how to make it better than I could, and a bit of bustle from customers, was an improvement.

It also meant my car was close by if I found something to follow up on.

I needed a link between Alan and Ivan, or a connection to Viktor, whatever his real name is. This time I had Glenda's phone and her unlock code.

I plugged in the charger and, while I waited for it to suck in enough juice to start up, did some research on the tricks and hidden apps that might be there.

One stood out. A tracker app that could be set to link two phones. Alan was just the type of guy who would stalk his wife that way.

It took a minute to find in all the downloads. Glenda didn't organize her tools in any kind of order I recognized. A different version than the one I found online, and it wouldn't work unless the phone was charged. But now, Alan might be looking at my location. I should take out the sim card and then give the device to Andy, or to David to pass on.

I've never been good at doing things simply because I should. I opened the app. If Alan came for me, I was safe here in public view. I would call for help if I even caught a glimpse of him.

It was a mutual tracking service. Glenda could have used it to locate Alan as much as he tracked her. Three phone numbers were listed. Glenda's, Alan's, and one I didn't recognize. I made a note and checked his current location. Nothing current, but the history interested me. He frequented about four places at night. The same ones I found on the transactions, but apparently, he didn't always pay a bill with his card. I looked them up to remind myself of what I'd seen before. One was the nightclub. One a residence, one I couldn't seem to find on Google maps, and the other his home.

I had two places to check out tonight. The one Google couldn't find was out at Lighthouse Park. That would need a team to search, and I didn't have one. And I wouldn't get away with giving the cops one place to look at while keeping the details of the others to myself.

I found more than I expected to find, and if Alan's phone was off, he didn't learn my location. Or maybe he tossed the thing. If he had, I wouldn't be able to track him live, but history would do for now.

One thing he would need is money. I tagged his credit card and checked his bank account. No withdrawals in the last day. I was tempted to transfer the balance to Glenda's account. She would need as much cash as possible to start her new life. I didn't do it, because it was a big risk. If he found out, he'd know Glenda survived, and he'd be angry. His temper was enough of a threat for me to back out. She had protection, but if he didn't learn where she was, no one would try to test it. I risked revealing Glenda's account to Andy by moving funds, too.

I ordered another latte and sat back to think. How smart was Alan? I mean, getting involved with Russian gangs wasn't a sign of intelligence, but as an investment adviser, he earned the credentials. No one handed those out for free. So, intelligent enough to pass exams, but I had no clue if he ever handled money for legitimate clients. His smarts concerned me more. Was it his idea to put the app on Glenda's phone? I opened up a database and typed in the unknown number from the tracker. A Toronto area code. They didn't have the capabilities of a smartphone, so how did the app work?

Nothing on Google, and I didn't expect there to be, but going into the dark net is something I needed to do at home, not through an open network. I dropped it into my to-do list and asked myself again, how smart is Alan?

When he's angry, not so much, but was the attack his idea? And did anger, craziness, or fear drive him?

I checked the history on the tracker again. Glenda told me where she thought he spent time, but that didn't mean she knew the truth.

According to the record, he'd been in North Vancouver at a restaurant that I could look up. Maybe someone would remember him and his companion. Just dropping by was likely going to get me nowhere. I looked up the place online. Great reviews. The chef was well known. No hints of problems or links to organized crime. But Yelp didn't have a category for drive-by shootings or drug deals.

Those were in the police records, and I had an in with them.

I called David but got his voicemail. I didn't leave a message because it's hard to wheedle without conversation. I would try later. The information didn't help me figure out how much Alan was being controlled, or if he was in a position to instigate anything. Although on second consideration, he must be a lackey because if he held any power, he would have sent someone else to batter his wife. Doing it himself guaranteed the cops would keep him away from her.

The phone was twenty percent charged so I pulled the plug and turned it off. As much as I didn't want to bunker down at home, I needed to move on.

I reached to shut down my laptop and noticed the alert on Alan's Visa card. He was spending money, and he was still in Vancouver. The charge was over on the east side. With luck, I'd make the drive in twenty minutes. I promised myself to call David again to report him if Alan was still there. If I was very lucky, he wasn't settling up a bar bill before leaving the place.

37

I made it to the place in good time. Alan's phone was still offline, which was all I could check in the moments at a red light. The credit card activity took more than a glance, so I decided not to risk a ticket for unsafe driving — or an accident.

The location was a restaurant that turned into more of a nightclub after nine p.m. This part of East Vancouver sat at the north end of The Drive. Still kind of funky and hipster-ish, but also fading into old warehouses and commercial outlets.

The area was historically an Italian enclave. This place stood out with its Cyrillic alphabet. I took a picture and dropped it into the translate app. Yup, Russian, *Sila*, meaning strength. I guess we don't use the same naming conventions as other cultures. Would I go to a restaurant called Strength? No. But what about *Forza*? It sounded better in Italian, so apparently some languages worked and some didn't.

Now that I was here, I realized I had no way to slide in

unrecognized. Alan knew me as an investigator, and the last time he saw me, he'd battered his wife and abandoned his child. I should have thought this through before barreling across the city. David was in a better position to do this. He could arrest Alan if I caught him in the place. But I didn't want to wait for him to arrive, and I wasn't going to call Andy.

Not an easy reconnaissance. Tinted windows so you couldn't see in unless you pressed your face to the glass. Unfortunately, since the tint only went one way, everyone inside had a clear view of the street, so my actions wouldn't fall under the definition of sneaking.

I left my car and strolled past the restaurant. If I found Alan's car, I'd call David. If I couldn't find it in the most obvious places, I'd risk going in.

Not in the parking lot in the alley, or any of the other business spots. Not high enough ranked to be afforded a reserved slot. Only a few other places to check; because of the warehouses, the residential streets mostly had permit parking restrictions. Not on the one where I parked, and not on the next one, or the third. I found plenty of spaces available in range, so I figured he'd gone.

I checked the records again, and no other transaction alerts.

I took a final look around as I got my mind ready to walk into what was very likely a mob restaurant. Then I noticed the five Harleys lined up at the sidewalk a block away. One of them I recognized: Guy.

I needed to get inside so he'd see me, and then leave so he would follow me and talk. I sent a small prayer out to the universe that Stick wasn't with him and opened the door.

No Stick, but five bikes outside and only four Angels inside kept me on edge.

Guy flicked a glance my way.

I walked up to the man standing at the end of the bar. "Hi, I'm lost. Do you know where *Fets* is?"

He looked at me, and I watched him decide to help rather than ignore me.

"South of here. On the other side of the street," he said.

I pulled out my phone and tapped *Fets* into the maps and showed it to him. "But it says it should be around here."

He let out a breath with a groan. Like I was too stupid to live. "Look at the compass." I turned it toward me, glared at it and laughed. "OMG, I'm sorry, I thought north was up. Got to go."

He simply blinked at me.

I turned to catch Guy's eye before heading back to the street.

HE JOINED me about thirty seconds later and dragged me around the corner. "You are going to get killed."

"For reading my GPS wrong?"

He didn't laugh.

"You're lucky Stick was in the can. Why are you here?"

I told him about Glenda and that I knew about Alan being in the restaurant. "I need to find him. Where did he go?"

"You mean you want to catch the head of the gang. Sure, you want Blackhouse punished, but you won't stop with him, right? Charity, you have a cop on call. Use him."

No point in pretending. "First, I need to get Alan off the street, so Glenda and the kid are safe. If I find some way to pull more gang members into custody, great. Just tell me what you know, and I'll make sure you aren't nearby when the shit hits."

"I give up." Guy cocked his head, listening for something. "Yeah, Blackhouse was here. He owed us for a shipment. That went through *Sila's* books. He's off to meet Viktor. I think he's trying to keep moving so no one can catch up. He's high, so be careful."

A link to Viktor? "Who is this Viktor guy?"

"You'll find out when you see him," Guy said. "Are you tracking Blackhouse's transactions?"

He was not good at actually giving up on me because he always followed the advice to stop with telling me what I wanted to know. "Yes."

"This is all dangerous, Charity. I am not going to make it easy for you to get killed, because I would feel bad about it. And your boyfriend would find me."

"He doesn't know about you."

He chuckled and then checked the street again. "Keep thinking that. Look. Where Blackhouse is going, he'll spend money. He's meeting Viktor and you'll get a good look at him. Don't go home because you'll need to be mobile."

If he told me who Viktor really was, I wouldn't be in danger, but maybe he would. I had no idea if the information could be tracked back to him. "Okay. How long do you think I'll be waiting?"

"He'll probably arrive in the next ten minutes. If you can be on the road while you get the credit card info, head east."

East was a big area and from here, I could be on the wrong side of the Fraser, and it was highway travel all the way, so no easy place to pull over to check once I started. And I would need to do that to check the credit card alert. "Okay. You sure he'll stay long enough for me to drive there?"

"He'll be waiting at least an hour for Viktor."

I thanked him and went to cross the road to my car. Guy pulled me back into the alley. "Look first," he said. "What if Stick came outside?"

He looked and then let my arm go. I rushed across the street and got in my car.

38

I t was getting late and if I was going to drive east, I'd be stuck in rush hour traffic. Guy said Alan would stick around for an hour at least, but if I didn't get his location soon, it could take longer for me to get there.

I'm not good with waiting at the best of times, and hanging around to receive the information I needed to barge into a dangerous situation stretched me to my limit. And if the notice came in the form of a transaction flag, Alan was paying, and people usually did that just before leaving.

I worried over what to do for long enough to see Guy and his pals leave *Sila* and rumble away. Then the lights went on outside the restaurant, bringing out the nightclub vibe.

I'd started plotting a route east that would provide a few places to stop and check messages before I crossed a river, when my phone pinged. Alan had turned his on. Thank God.

He was at another night club, in Coquitlam, a destination which wasn't on the route I planned. Somehow, waiting gave me luck. I didn't expect that fact to make anything easier in the future.

I headed for the Trans-Canada, praying there would be no accidents. The traffic would be heavy, but as long as the cars moved, I would make it. If I had to take an early exit, I'd be on a road with a lot of streetlights.

Luck was still with me, and I pulled up in a parking space across the way from the nightclub twenty minutes later. Not sure why a bar would open before ten p.m., but this one was. The occasional well-muscled man strolled in from the street. And a couple of them huddled in a corner smoking. This was going to be impossible if the place was full of men.

That made me think. I didn't need to do this on my own. Well, I did want to be the one to catch Alan, but I could call for backup. I sent David a text to contact me.

Five minutes later he did. I'd had time to think about what I needed to say.

"I'm sorry," I said. "I've been stupid and stubborn."

"So, you want me to call Andy for you? You should do it, Charity."

"No, I was apologizing to you." I'd bring Andy in when I had something for him, not before. "I'm following a lead, and it's brought me to a nightclub. In Coquitlam. Called, *Vecherinka*."

"Ivan Kuznetsov's hangout. It's under surveillance."

He didn't say the words 'get out' but I heard them anyway. "They are not doing a great job. Alan is inside."

"Don't go in until I call back," he said. "Andy needs to hear about what's happening, or you might be pulled out by his team."

"Alan isn't going to be there long," I said. "I'm not losing him, and he's meeting the adoption guy. I'm going in whether Andy likes it or not."

He paused long enough that I wondered if I was on hold. I picked out background sounds, so maybe he was getting his patience together so he wouldn't yell.

"David?"

"I'll tell him that. Will you wait?"

"You've got fifteen minutes."

He didn't waste any of it saying goodbye. I spent my time watching the door to *Vecherinka*. I checked Google Translate: Party.

Two women entered alone. Both dressed for business, not partying. The club served as someone's office, maybe Kuznetsov. A couple more men went in, five came out and the smokers finished up and headed in.

My phone rang. "What did he say?"

"He knew Alan was there. They aren't prepared to blow the case to arrest him."

"Do they have anything against Kuznetsov? I mean, something they are about to act on?"

"I don't know. And I'm not going to ask. They won't stop you, but he asked if you would record what's going on."

So, it's not too dangerous for me to do that? "No. I'll get caught. My plan is to go in and pretend to be surprised I find Alan there. I'll stall him or follow him. Right now, he's my only problem."

"Will you wait for me? You need someone who can arrest the guy. Not a good idea in the club, but we can take him when he heads outside."

"I need to do this myself," I said. "I know I can't arrest him, but if you come with me, they'll peg you as a cop."

He didn't answer.

"Are you coming now?" I asked into the void.

"Yes. I promise I won't get in the way of you doing your thing."

I hated putting him in this position. He knew how much of a risk I took going into the club. He probably had more information about what went on in there than I did — no, make that he certainly did. But Alan met me as a PI, not as a cop's girlfriend. He wouldn't be threatened. And I could pretend I hadn't seen what he'd done to Glenda.

"Okay," I said. "I can't wait for you to get here, but I'll text you confirmation if Alan is still there. If I say something like tell Glenda he's here, you'll know Kuznetsov is inside too."

I told him where I'd parked, and I loved him. The last part just popped out. I guess I was more worried about what happened than I thought.

"Love you, too. I'll be with you in twenty," he said. "I'm on lights and sirens most of the way."

It was kind of sexy to have a boyfriend who could do that. And one who didn't get all weird about what I said.

Twenty minutes. I would wait another ten before I went in, but I wasn't sitting here until David arrived. It would help me if I only needed to bluff for a short time. I'm not sure how long I could keep the memory of Glenda's body on the floor from pushing my temper over the top. And if Viktor did show up? Well, I'd figure out a way to have him arrested too.

39

Inside, it wasn't what I expected. I'm a bit embarrassed to admit it, but I imagined something overly ornate; lots of gold, red velvet, and mirrors. It was done out in soft gray tones and deep blue accents. The atmosphere carried a little menace, but nothing overt.

Alan sat at a table about halfway down the dance floor, talking on his phone. He didn't see me right away because he was turned to say something to a man who was heading to the back of the room.

A tall man, blond, built. From the back I had no idea how old.

The various groups I'd seen enter were scattered at tables, drinking and talking. No redhead of any kind. They paid no attention to me, but I'd bet my fee I was under surveillance.

I marched toward Alan getting two steps away before he turned and saw me. If he was that confident of the security in the room that he forgot to take care of his own safety, I had a chance; egos are great leverage.

"What are you doing in here?" He dropped his phone on the table and stood from the chair as he asked. I took the action as an invitation to join him.

In my head I tried to keep track of how long it would be before I could expect David. It was hard because my nerves kept twisting my perception. "I came looking for you," I said. "I'm a PI, remember?"

"Yeah, but your clients must have made a decision by now." He waved to the bartender for another drink. By the size of his pupils, he should be avoiding any kind of mind-altering substance.

I abandoned my plan about Glenda's injuries. Offense might get me further here. "Your wife is going to be fine by the way," I said. "Nora's okay, too."

He got control fast, but I noticed the little flinch before he schooled his expression. "What do you mean?"

I could use that denial to stretch out the conversation. Two minutes must have passed by now. "You don't know?"

Some people are very good at lying under pressure with no delay to think something up. Alan wasn't one of them. He avoided answering by calling out to the bartender to hurry up. A few of the men around the other tables smirked.

This was a good seat. I didn't need to turn much to check the entrance. I could see to the back of the room in case blond guy came back, and there were two groups of what I can only think of as henchmen behind him. So, their reactions might be useful in my evil plans to detain Alan. Unfortunately for him, they didn't hold a high opinion of their money launderer.

The drink arrived, a martini, and Alan took a sip while he got his story together. "What? The last time I saw her, you and your clients were bothering her."

Not a bad effort. "And you rushed us out, why? You have something to hide?"

"Glenda doesn't know about the way we got Nora. I told you that."

I shrugged. Sometimes indifference can prompt a response.

"Did you tell her?" he asked. "It won't make a difference now. The kid is hers."

"She's smarter than you give her credit for." Part of me wanted to call him all kinds of asshole for beating his wife, but that would tip him off, get me thrown out — at minimum — and not help the situation. Going along with his pretense that he left her in good shape might help me more. "But, no, I didn't tell her anything."

"What did you mean by she's okay?" He brought us back to the beginning. "I left her sitting on the couch. Nora was asleep."

Surely, David was almost here. I'm not sure how long the henchmen would find me entertaining. "She's in the hospital."

"How do you know that?"

Not 'what happened,' which is the normal question. "I dropped back to see if she was okay. She seemed pretty tense when you came back in. I found her unconscious in a pool of blood."

"Someone must have broken in," he said.

Not 'which hospital?' Did he even notice how little he cared?

"I got back there fast," I said. No need to mention the RCMP surveillance. "You didn't stick around long."

"I'm a busy guy."

The back door cracked open, and I caught a glimpse of the blond man. I didn't catch many details, but his hair was only thick on the back. From the front, he was bald. High cheekbones with no excess fat to soften them. One of the henchmen stepped up, said something in his ear, and the door closed.

"Are you too busy to visit your wife?" It might be better to send him off to be arrested at the hospital. But that put Glenda in danger. If Alan visited, it would be to finish the job, not bring a get-well present.

"Yes. You said she was okay, so no need to rush over. She needs the rest."

Now, David should be walking through the door any second. No matter how my fear screwed up my sense of time, it had been long enough. "I'm headed to her next," I said. "I'll tell her you'll be by later."

Alan looked around the room, maybe thinking about how it looked for him to be talking to a strange woman in the gang hideout. No one met his eye. He didn't ask for help — not a good idea to show that you weren't man enough to take on a woman in this company.

Then I heard the bar phone go. The room became tense. The bartender answered it, said something quietly and then nodded to the closest henchman.

"Don't make any promises," Alan said.

I had to work hard to keep my attention on him because something was happening. Something Alan didn't notice.

With no fuss or noise, the bar started to empty. Why didn't Alan join the exodus? They couldn't afford to let him be arrested, and that call could only have been something on the lines of 'cheese it the cops.'

Now there was only one henchman sitting behind Alan. I turned to check the space behind me. Only one on that side, too.

This might easily end up with both of us on our knees

waiting for the two bullets to the head that ended us as risks.

Alan finally realized something was up and swore, then stood ready to leave. "You brought the cops?"

40

"No." I figured a lie would keep things under some form of control until David came in. But I needed to drag more out of Alan, incriminating evidence, not just denials and silence. "Maybe they're here because of the people who hang out in the club." Unfortunately, also scaring off anyone who arrived now: like Viktor.

"You don't understand how dangerous this is," he said. Then he sat. "How long before they arrive?"

"I haven't a clue. But you know what? I don't care if the cops are on their way. It seems like everyone but you got the warning. What are these two guys still doing here?"

He didn't look up from his empty glass. "To kill me if I talk."

So, he did understand how little they valued him. If I ran an organization that needed specific skills, like money laundering, I would make sure I had back-up plans. Ivan was most likely getting his number two accountant to clear the funds and history to someplace safe.

"You think they will kill you even if you don't talk?"

"Look, I can't tell you anything. What I know points only

to me. And even if I knew more, you wouldn't be able to protect me."

He didn't mention Glenda. She would need protection regardless of what Alan did.

"I don't believe you." I kept my focus on the two henchmen reflected in the bar mirror. I had no idea what I would do if they reached for guns, but I couldn't let them surprise me with a bullet. "If you don't want to talk, I'll ask Glenda to tell me. The wife always knows more than the husband thinks she does."

"I hid everything from her. The boss was clear on that topic. You can't trust anyone with information."

"Even you?" I nodded my chin to the closest henchman. "Even them?"

Alan finally looked up at me. "You think the people left to avoid arrest?"

Exactly what I thought. His question made me rethink, but if I could get him talking about this, maybe he'd slip out something to use. "Why else?"

"Half of them probably went to the boss. One of them hustled the women away, but the big guy needs protection. The rest are out on the street slowing your back-up down with questions and demands. By the time they make it inside, there'll be nothing to find."

So possibly an office in the back. Computers and files were flowing out the back of the building. "Why haven't they done anything?" I nodded again to the henchmen who just sat at their tables, effectively blocking my access to an exit. "Am I a hostage?"

He laughed. Not the kind of patronizing sound that meant I was too stupid to figure it out — hysterical. I waited for him to take control, but he couldn't. Whatever he was on pushed him past his ability to control his emotions. How much could I do to him before henchies acted? I got up, went to the bar and asked for a pint of cold water.

Alan gasped for air, and each breath sounded more like a sob than a laugh. I threw the water in his face. He stopped panting and swung at me.

I expected the reaction and ducked. The henchman in the back rose from his seat. Alan took control. Henchman sat again.

We were being held here for a reason. If they wanted us dead, we'd already be on the floor in a pool of blood and brains. My instinct was right. They wanted us here as hostages — or maybe they wanted me for that. Alan's punishment would come without witnesses.

"So, I guess the answer is yes," I said when Alan finished wiping his face. "What makes you so valuable?"

"The guy who runs this organization isn't a dumb crook. He's smart and patient. If I'm dead, he can't use me. So as long as I don't totally screw up, I'll be fine. Telling you anything falls into the 'kill him fast' column. I'm here to keep you occupied. To stop you from rushing out and causing more problems."

How could I have gotten it so wrong? The clues were there. He didn't care at all about Glenda. His fear was all in my head. He had something on the boss that kept him alive — for now. But I was a pain in the ass. Why did he keep me alive?

I asked Alan that question.

"Killing you brings more trouble. He'll find a way to make you compliant if he can't force you to work for him. If you want my guess?"

"Sure, why not?"

"You behave right now. When it's over, you stop whatever this investigation is about, and you'll be left alone."

"And Glenda? Nora?"

"Glenda doesn't know anything. So, if she starts talking, no way she can do any harm." He looked at the henchman behind us. "Go see what's happening."

Henchie did as ordered.

I am so stupid. I was never in control. He probably led me here by turning on the phone. I needed rescuing, and that pissed me off.

I turned around to check what would happen when Henchie returned. It didn't take long; he backed through the entrance hands up, closely followed by a cop in riot armor.

David came in behind the officer and strode over when he saw me.

"You are in so much trouble." He pulled me in close, and for a second, for that tiny amount of time, I didn't care that I'd screwed up.

"Sorry," I said, and then wriggled out of his arms and stepped away. I wanted to witness Alan's arrest.

But Alan wasn't there. Sometime between me turning to see the big rescue and the cop walking in, he left.

"He was here," I said. "Alan. I have a lot to pass on to you, but he's not a dupe."

"You can tell Andy," David said. "He won't be put off any longer."

"Fine. Call him," I said. I needed David busy with something before he noticed what I'd just seen. Alan's phone. On the floor under the table, the burner he'd been using when I came in.

"Wait here while we get organized," David said. "Do you need anything?"

"I'm okay." As soon as his back turned, I swooped the phone into my pocket.

41

"**A**ndy is on his way," David said. "Do you know where Alan went?"

"No. I would tell you if I did. And thanks for rescuing me." I figured it was a good idea to say it before we had our next disagreement. The argument was coming up since I wasn't going to hang around to be yelled at by Andy for blowing a perfectly good surveillance location. No one would be chatting over a drink here about nefarious acts in the future.

Although, he should be thanking me for giving him a reason to come inside and get two henchmen who might talk for the right deal. And a bartender who wasn't innocent, because he'd issued the warning. Maybe all of them would keep him and his boss happy for a while.

"I need to leave. Can I give you my statement and head out? I'll be available for questioning later."

He looked at me long enough that I figured he planned to say no, and I had to stay. I didn't even try to pretend I was too upset to stay. It would have confirmed his suspicion I was hiding something. And I told myself I'd hand over the phone as soon as I had a chance to check out any clues.

"Did you learn anything?" he asked.

"Alan is deeper in than we thought. He dropped the victim act pretty quick when I confronted him. Some big shot left just after I sat down. When I thought they'd abandoned him, or were planning on executing him, I was wrong. The two guys you arrested were there to make sure he was safe." I blurted everything out, getting control of my mouth before I blabbed about the phone.

"What did the big shot look like?" David waved over one of the cops who were guarding the henchmen.

I told him and his face hardened. "Maybe Kuznetsov. Anyone else?"

I tried to think about the faces in the crowd when I entered. I'd hoped to find Viktor and so I really didn't pay attention to any man who didn't look like the photo with his wife. "No one I recognized."

He turned to the cop who was waiting patiently for orders. "When she leaves, make sure she gets to her car and watch her drive away."

He nodded and went to stand beside the door.

"Anyone interesting in the crowd outside?" I believed Alan when he said the others had been distracting the cops.

"No. We have pictures, but no reason to hold them." He waved to a team of people who walked in carrying plastic bins.

"Andy is going to let you search the place?" Maybe there was still something to find, but I doubted it.

"These are his team," David said. "They need to collect the surveillance devices, and they have a warrant."

"You got the warrant because I was here?" That was

something I could use when Andy attacked. "So, some good came of it."

"Unless we find something to prove our case against them, it's not much help," he said. Then he took a deep breath before pulling me into another hug. "It might have gone so wrong. You need to tell me what's going on before you jump into the tiger's cage."

I relaxed in his arms for a moment, feeling some of the adrenaline rush drain from me. Then he let me go. "I should tell you something."

That didn't sound like good news. "I'm being arrested for interfering in an investigation?" I tried to make it a joke, but it was a real possibility.

"Not yet, but you do need to make peace with Andy."

Why was he stalling? I needed to get out of here. The phone was tempting me, and I wanted to be gone long before Andy arrived. "Was that it?"

"No. I've been seconded to the RCMP investigation."

No clue in his voice or on his face whether it was a good thing or not. "And?"

"I think it was partly because of you," he said. "No, don't get angry. They didn't ask for me in a bid to control you. We needed a liaison, and I'm the right guy for that."

"Because you've learned how to handle me?" For some reason it didn't make me want to run.

"More likely because I know you enough not to try to handle you." He grinned, bringing a laugh out of me. "See, it works."

It might give me an in too, but I didn't want David's career to be hindered by my actions. "Is it a good move?"

"Yes and no. I'm not planning to join them permanently, but this is a big investigation. I'll get credit. It won't hurt me if we fail."

"We won't," I said. "I guess I could be more cooperative. Get you a giant gold star when they take Alan in."

He brushed his fingers down my arm and leaned in to whisper, "Don't do anything crazy. I prefer you in our bed, not a hospital."

Well, that made me all warm and tingly. But it didn't stop me from keeping the phone a secret. He was after the leaders of the gang. I just wanted Alan, and Viktor. I couldn't help thinking Nora had been lucky and some of the kids they sold were living a hell. "I'll see you tonight, but now I need to go."

I kissed his cheek and walked away.

The cop followed me through the door and across the street to my car. He stopped me from getting in until he checked the underside of the car and looked in the back seat. When I opened the door, he made me pop the hood and looked again. I didn't think anyone had time to rig a bomb, but I was only counting from the time they knew about the cops. I'd given them plenty of time during the whole visit.

He lifted my trunk, slammed it closed, and nodded for me to go ahead.

Now that he'd verified the car was safe, my nerves took over with the worry he'd missed something. Five minutes ago, I couldn't wait to get away. Now, I had to force myself to start the ignition.

The car started; no one blew up.

42

A s soon as I was out of sight of my cop protection, I pulled over. The problem with suppressing the reaction to that much potential danger was it didn't go away. All the feelings came out when you least expected and at the least convenient time. Driving was a bad idea.

I sat in a mall parking lot at the back, no one parked nearby, no one wandering around looking for trouble. So, a great place to sit waiting out the shakes or whatever was coming my way. If the reaction didn't come in the next half hour, I would be good until much later. At least I hoped so because this case was moving pretty fast.

I needed to find Alan again. This time I wouldn't be under the illusion he was some kind of stooge. I'd be calling in Andy and David, and anyone who would come with guns and handcuffs. The phone was my way in. As long as I could crack the password.

I pulled it out and pressed the power button — fully charged, waiting for a code.

This wasn't the place to start stabbing at keys. I dropped it in my bag.

The guy who left early might be Ivan Kuznetsov. Andy must have a better picture of him than he'd shown me. I'd have to make nice with him to get a look. My priority was Alan, so nice could wait unless Andy forced the issue.

Viktor. Was he there? The social media posts and Guy's comments about the decoy made me confident that I knew what he looked like. I closed my eyes and let my mind float back. The lighting in the place was good enough for me to see Alan when I went in; I could have picked out a guy with Ivan's features. So, if I saw anyone I recognized, it should be in my memory.

I remember the impression of a lot of blond men. Viktor was red haired. I didn't see him. That didn't mean he wasn't lurking in the back room with Ivan.

My phone pinged. David had sent an image. I opened it. A blurry picture of a man, three quarter turned to the camera. A little clearer than before.

That's the guy. Ivan?

Yes, but you are supposed to be driving home.

Stopped for coffee.

Go home.

I sent a smiling emoji and put my phone down. He'd gotten the image from Andy. And fast, too. Maybe there were advantages to working with the RCMP.

My hand trembled, and my chest started to tighten. Apparently, I needed to know I'd been that close to a Russian mob leader to finally feel scared enough to react.

NO TEARS THIS TIME, but it took an hour before I felt steady enough to drive. I headed home, not because David told me

to, or not only because of that, but to get to my various pass-
word-cracking and people-tracking tools.

43

I got home and turned the coffee pot on, took a shower because I felt like I was covered in stress sweat, and then sat at my table wondering where to start.

I put the phone on to charge because it had lost half of the battery life since I dumped it in my bag. I closed my eyes so my mind could figure out the best thing to do with this opportunity before I handed it to the authorities. I promised I would do that as soon as I found something.

A burner wouldn't give me much. I needed Alan's actual phone. Not the one he used with Glenda, but the one he kept track of all his criminal activity on. No way I would get my hands on that. I could use his computer, but ditto on the odds of it being made available.

David would be tied up for hours with the investigation, so I didn't need to worry about interruptions. What I needed to worry about was my own inability to start.

If I couldn't get into Alan's records the easy way, I would be forced to go in the sneaky way. The phone was a good place to start. I had enough of his passwords and usernames from Glenda to work out his pattern. Everyone had a pattern.

The phone would probably lock if I tried the wrong code too many times, but I had to start with something. I entered the password she gave me for his personal phone. The idiot used the same one on the burner. I checked the call and text history — you'd think he would be ordered to clear it, but either no one thought to tell him, or he ignored the order because the data was all there. Nothing obviously incriminating, but a bunch of other numbers, likely burners, and, even better, a series of texts about meetings.

I got that tingle in the base of my brain that told me I was heading somewhere. I made a note of all the numbers and the contents of the texts. Maybe later I would find a pattern. And I would have to hand it over to David pretty quickly, so having my own record of the calls would be a good idea.

It was late, and I couldn't make the tickle of a plan blossom. My body wanted to sleep, but my mind ran too fast to rest, or think properly. I promised myself a half hour of work, then I'd take some down time and let my subconscious deal with the details.

I hit repeat on the thirty-minute timer, and an hour later it was getting harder to think of the next steps. Despite my brain racing, my eyelids drooped. Time to try a nap.

I crawled into bed in my clothes. As soon as my head hit the pillow, all traces of drowsiness vanished. Damn it.

I rolled over on my side, trying not to tense up. I did some breathing exercises and kept my eyes closed. Sleep found its way and my brain let me go.

. . .

THE SOUND of car horns woke me up in the wee hours. A party leaving one of the buildings across the street from the marina. I'd slept for four hours. Too early to go knocking on doors, and I had no idea what doors would be worth knocking on yet.

I showered and did the usual morning things because I wasn't going back to sleep. This case couldn't drag on for much longer. If I didn't find something today, all the leads would be too stale to follow.

My subconscious had done its job. I didn't need Alan's laptop. I needed to find what cloud storage he used. He would have details and evidence to use if he tried to make a deal. And since he didn't have the smarts to create different passwords for his phone, I could probably figure out how to log into his account.

I put the coffee on and started searching for accounts. I entered his business email for the user because he'd be able to write off the cost that way. I had his laptop password and an idea of how he came up with new ones. And cloud services didn't block you after a few unsuccessful tries.

There are lots of services, but I started with the big three. His laptop was a Windows machine, I headed over to the Microsoft cloud, typed in his email and laptop password. No joy.

What email would he use? How stupid was he with computer security? Could it be the password?

I poured a cup of coffee and thought while I made toast. Yes, I could just keep trying things that popped into my head, but that wasn't a good approach. I needed to keep track of what I tried because I couldn't afford to waste hours if I didn't hit lucky. What did I know about Alan? He likely didn't set up the computer himself. He might not understand about the cloud backup. So, he wouldn't have created the sign-in credentials.

I sat down, sent a prayer out to whoever managed the rules of luck and typed the email address again, then ADMIN123. A basic password he would have been told to change immediately.

But he hadn't.

And I had thousands of files that I was sure Alan didn't know existed. I stared at the screen, wondering where to start.

A lot of the folders had numeric names that I couldn't interpret, at least without some thought. These would be what Andy needed. Somewhere would be a link to Kuznetsov's money. I would find out if the cops required a warrant before I sent along the link. I pulled out my box of thumb drives and backup hard drives, none of them big enough to hold the contents of Alan's cloud files.

At the bottom of the list were about fifty folders with names. None of them were Ivan Kuznetsov or Evil Gang Boss and his money laundering adventures.

But two of them jumped off the screen.

McCarthy V and Gupta.

I had what I needed to find Viktor. But he would come second. Gupta was the name of the foster mother.

I opened the folder and started reading, hoping it was a coincidence.

Ten minutes later I was running for my car and texting David and Andy to call me. I'd let the big guns do the work now.

44

I arrived outside the foster home in record time; not much traffic at two a.m. What I should have seen was a quiet street with few lights on inside houses. The Gupta home was lit up like there was a party going on. No music, no loud voices, so no complaints from the neighbors.

Andy's surveillance team probably reported on unusual activity. I had no idea what was normal for this time in the morning. What I did know is kids were in the house. Someone needed to protect them, and the RCMP might not think of that in the rush to catch a big player.

As I sat trying to figure out how to deal with what I learned, Alan drove up.

He parked in the driveway, stepped out and didn't even look around before marching up the steps and opening the door like he lived there.

I called Andy. I didn't care if he already knew about Alan; I needed to find out what was going on. I wanted them to know I was inside in case they came in guns blazing.

"Charity?" Andy answered on the first ring.

"I'm at the foster house. Alan is here."

"How do you know?"

I could hear talking in the background. He was working, just like me.

"I saw him walk into the house. Where is your surveillance?" Had he pulled it when they got to the club? "Where are you?"

"I'm on my way. Are you hidden from anyone looking out?"

Nice of him to be concerned, but that wouldn't stop me. "For now. Where are your guys?"

"I'm bringing David and a team. Wait for us. I don't want you doing something stupid."

"Something like leaving the foster house unprotected?" He had no right to make me feel bad about being here. I found the evidence he needed to arrest someone in the gang. I called to tell him. And he didn't answer my question. "How long before you get here?"

"The team is in place," he said. "I'll reach out on my way to see why they aren't reporting. How did you know to go to the house?"

"How long until you arrive?" My evidence would keep for now. It wasn't something I could explain quickly — okay, it was, but I needed to make sure he didn't arrest me for taking the phone because he'd find a way to make it a problem.

"Twenty," he said. "If I don't hear from my team, I'm going to check them first. Hang on."

A long pause while I watched the front door of the house. No one came out, no one else went in. The blinds were down on the windows, so I couldn't gather information by observation. If David or Andy didn't arrive in twenty minutes, I was going in. I'd make some noise to give people a chance to hide if they didn't want to be seen.

"Charity?" David's voice replaced Andy. "We're on the way. Please don't take any risks."

"The Guptas are connected," I said. "Wasn't Alan on some kind of list? Shouldn't alarms have gone off when he arrived?"

"What made you go there?" he asked. "You aren't sitting outside that house at this time in the morning for no reason."

"I had an idea that panned out," I said. He was being too rational. I was missing something. Was he pissed that I had done something to invalidate any evidence and blow the case? "I'll give Andy everything when he gets here. But does his warrant cover information in the cloud?"

He asked and I heard Andy confirm, but they hadn't been able to break into the laptop yet.

"As soon as we arrive," David said, "you give him everything, right?"

There was still something bothering him. "Yes. I mean. I don't have everything, I think. I didn't have time to open the files. I saw the foster parents' names and came here."

"Promise me you'll sit tight."

This was stupid. If anything happened to make me think the kids were in danger, I was going in. But the surveillance team would know, and they would cover me.

"Yes, unless someone comes out with a kid under each arm, or the house starts burning I will wait. Why are you so worried? I'm not going to put myself at risk for nothing. The guys watching in the utility van will come in if things go bad."

Another long pause and my mind shifted like someone shunted it into another direction.

"There's something wrong in the van." David spoke quietly. He didn't sound too scared, but I knew him. He was trying to keep it together. Andy was sitting next to him, driving and freaking out about his surveillance team.

"It's still here," I said. "I'll go look."

"No," he shouted the word. "Stay in the car."

I stepped out and closed the door as silently as possible. "I'll only knock on the door. Maybe their communications are down."

"Leave it to us," David said, his voice tight.

"No. I don't want Andy crashing the car because he's trying to get here too fast. No one is on the street. The house is closed up and no one is watching. If I can't look in, they can't look out, right?"

I approached the van from the opposite sidewalk just in case I was wrong. I checked over my shoulder before running across the street to the back of the truck. "I'm here. Nothing looks out of place. They should know I'm at the door, right?"

"Yes. Maybe they think you'll go away if they ignore you. Go ahead and knock."

As I stood there, all kinds of scenarios floated to my mind. Whoever was at the Guptas' felt safe enough to meet there. They must know the cops would be watching. Did they take out the team inside? I took a breath and then banged on the door.

"No response. Should I open it?"

I could hear Andy yelling something, but David answered, "Yes."

I grabbed the ring that served as a handle. "Locked."

"Wait for us. Don't go back to the car. We are almost with you."

I couldn't sit here not knowing if the people inside needed help, waiting a vague amount of time. 'Almost there' could be fifteen minutes. I banged on the door again and put my ear against the metal.

"I hear movement." I checked the street and slipped around to the driver's side. The windows were darkened out and a bit too high. But the back door had no keyhole, so I had nothing to work on.

Fuck! The door was the same. And this kind of truck didn't have a passenger door. "Is there some way to release the lock remotely?"

"No. They are alive, and you need to hide and wait."

"Okay. Hurry."

45

I t's not in my nature to sit idle and wait for help. Going into the house would break my promise, and I wasn't willing to take that risk with my relationship — the one with David as a man or the one with him as a cop. From my seat on the curb next to the truck, I could still peek at the house. Nothing had changed, so no immediate threat.

I pulled out my phone and went into the files on Alan's cloud. Not ideal, but it was all I had.

Before I dug in, I sent a text to remind David and Andy to bring Child Services to take care of the kids. No matter what happened in that house, the Guptas were not a safe haven.

Once again, I wished for Alan's personal phone. One that would have lots of lovely pictures and texts and a call log. I didn't have it, and there was no file called burner backup in the list.

I looked at McCarthy_V, a bunch of documents all with what looked like random numbers and dates as the name. Cursing my phone's lack of ability to open multiple files, I opened the first one and found a full page of garbled text.

The same happened for the next four. So, they were encrypted. The RCMP could do the work on that. I went back to the top-level file list and clicked the view options. A few photos, but no picture with the gang all labeled clearly with a menu of crimes committed.

Doing a search on the directory was useless on the phone. Too hard to read the results.

I wouldn't have much longer to dig into this information. As soon as Andy arrived, he would demand it and I'd be cut off. I should have saved a copy in my own cloud account before I came, but I was in a rush to get here — and wait.

The reason Alan kept the files was obvious. Ammunition to get a deal when everything went wrong. Whether that included his wife and kid was anyone's guess. It also meant he wasn't as stupid as people seemed to think. He would have kept transaction records and transcripts of conversations, and...

This time I didn't need to open a file. I just needed see if they were there. I searched for wav files. Yes, he had recordings. Mov and MP4 too. Almost as if he was a mole for the cops. I beat the suspicion back. No one would let him off the hook for buying a kid and beating his wife half to death. It would screw up any prosecution.

My next steps were interrupted by a text from Andy, I guessed David typing under orders.

Ten minutes

You need to hand over everything you have

And you need to account for every second you've held onto evidence

Sorry

The last came from David, not dictated by Andy.

So, in the next five minutes to be safe, I needed to figure out what else Alan had in the directory. Smart enough to keep this information; Stupid enough not to change his password. He was smart enough to encrypt it, and stupid enough to...

I typed Key into the search box. A bunch of the encrypted files showed up and one worksheet. Yep, stupid enough to keep the decryption key right with the coded information.

Before I tried to decode some of the information, I peeked at the house. Not as bright as before, the lights were out on the upper floor. I wanted to do more poking around before I lost control of the data to Andy. I opened the worksheet. It asked me to enter the text to decrypt. Crap. Copy and paste didn't work all the time on the phone.

I went back to one of the Gupta documents, said a prayer, and copied the contents, then pasted the whole thing into the indicated space on the spreadsheet. When I clicked the run button another box popped up with the results. A list of names with dollar amounts and dates. Definitely something Andy could use. I shut down everything.

I strained to hear the sound of a speeding car, but nothing. What I heard was worse, someone shouting in the foster house. Alan. A very angry Alan.

I put my phone in my pocket with my other devices and keys, and ran for the door.

46

Running into a building full of angry mobsters when the cops were on their way was a new high in stupidity for me. But the kids needed someone in the situation with their protection as the only priority — and they needed me there now. Not after I explained everything to Andy: now.

I barreled through the door ready to fight anyone in my way. No one stood in my way.

Alan and a man I figured was Manjeet Gupta faced off in the living room. They weren't yelling any longer. It was going to be a matter of seconds before that changed. And the wrong word would flick this to violence in a flash. No guns in sight, no kids, no Prem.

I was in the hyper alert state that sped up my perceptions of the situation. It must have been a real survival instinct when facing down a large predator, and the options were limited to attack, freeze, or flee. This needed more complex decisions, and that's where instinct fell short. I'd run into the house, so fleeing didn't make any sense. Freezing would make me dead pretty fast. And I could only attack with my witty repartee. That was shut down at the moment.

"What's going on?" The words got their attention. I hoped the interruption to their building testosterone would deescalate the tension enough for my brain to kick back in.

"Who are you?" Gupta asked.

"How did you get in here?" Alan asked at the same time.

"The door was open," I said. "I heard you yelling."

The questions seemed to calm the situation. I guess it's hard to escalate an argument if something distracts you. I wasn't happy the interruption seemed to bond them against a common threat — me. And I'd stupidly turned off my phone before charging in, so I wasn't recording anything.

Alan stepped to join Manjeet blocking my access into the rest of the house. "It's not even three a.m. You usually hang out on residential streets at this time of day?"

"When I'm worried about someone, I don't sleep." I didn't want to get into why Alan was here and how he got into the house yet. I only needed to hold their attention for a few minutes. David would be here with me even if Andy had to ask for permission to enter.

"You can go now," Gupta said. "This is fine, all under control. A little disagreement between friends. Come back tomorrow and talk to the wife."

"I'd like to make sure Nora is safe," I said. "And the other kids."

Alan took a step toward me. "She isn't alone. Isn't that right? You are working with the cops. Those ones in the van."

Manjeet grabbed Alan's arm. "What van?"

I kept my mouth shut.

"The feds have been watching the house for days. I took

care of them an hour ago. They should have been looking out the back, not just at your door."

"You killed them?" Gupta asked. "The boss said no cops unless he gave the order."

"I know what he said." Alan pulled out of Manjeet's grip. "I only immobilized them. By the time they get free, we'll be gone."

Gone? If they were planning on disappearing, what was the fight about?

"No," Manjeet said. "We can't simply walk away. It will take time to get our hands on the money and the files."

"You came here for your escape fund?" I asked. All the data must not be in the cloud. That would only take a few minutes to copy and delete. Paper files? And the money? Surely Alan had access to hidden accounts.

"You wanted to see Nora?" Prem's voice made me turn to the other door in the room. She held an almost sleeping Nora by the hand. "Here she is."

Suddenly, priorities changed. It was up to the real cops to find information. I needed Nora. All the kids of course, but Nora was here. "Come over here, Nora." I reached out my hand.

She started moving, then Prem grabbed her back and pulled another kid forward, a boy.

"If you go, they will be okay," she said. "We'll be gone, and you can do what you want with them."

I couldn't take her word I'd find the children alive if I walked away now. "Let me take all the kids now. I'll go and you can just pack up and leave."

Alan ran to the front door and locked it. "No. She stays with us. Easier to use as a hostage than the brats."

Oh, great work Charity, being a hostage is much better than being the person who solves the case.

"Look, you don't need the kind of trouble we'll make," I said, holding my hands out to the kids. "Let me take all the children. No one to slow you down. You get away and the children are safe. They don't know anything. They are too young to be used against you. I don't have anything the cops can use. You are in the clear right now. Don't mess that up."

47

"No!" Alan screamed. He wasn't thinking straight any longer. That sound carried fear along with the rage, and it was all pointed at me. "The kids stay. You stay. The cops will be here any minute, right?"

"What do you mean?" Prem asked. "Why would they come?"

"She called them," Manjeet said, "before she broke in."

Letting them talk it out wasn't lowering the tension as I'd hoped. If I couldn't get the potential hostages, including me, away, I needed to remove the kids from the direct action.

"Even if she was stupid enough to come in without back-up," Alan said, "those guys in the van should be reporting in on a regular schedule. I intended to be long gone before they were missed. At least they aren't behind her."

"You knew they were there?" I asked. Not the most insightful question given the team was tied up or something, but I needed back in the conversation. "How long?"

Alan grinned. "You all thought you were so smart. Since day one. The boss told us to leave them. No one was in danger if they kept looking here."

"He left us as goats?" Prem screamed. "He told us we would be taken care of if everything went to shit."

Nora started whimpering as I worked my way through what she'd said.

"If your husband had followed orders, you would be fine. But he had to try to be the big man. Had to ask for more money." Alan took a step toward Prem.

She backed away. "Can you shut her up?" She nodded in my direction.

No guns in sight. Still, three against one and a couple of scared children meant I needed a weapon. No handy candlestick to use as a bat, no heavy ornaments to throw. I liked my chances better with Prem. She might be easier to take down, and I'd be close to the kids if I succeeded. Where the hell was the cavalry?

I took a step between her and Alan. If she thought I was protecting her, I might get an edge.

"Look, this isn't going to end well at all. I didn't call the cops, and maybe the people in the van weren't supposed to check in for a while yet. If you keep yelling, a neighbor is going to phone in a noise complaint."

"I don't care," Alan said. "I have a job to do, and then I'm gone."

He was the money guy, not an assassin. Unless he was being tested. Or thrown away. Kuznetsov might just be cleaning house. Send Alan to get rid of the Guptas, and take Alan out right after.

Prem pushed Nora toward Alan, but the kid tried to come to me. "Take her. Then you can go. Hurry, before the police come."

He recoiled. "I don't want her. I want the money I left here. The cash."

His running stash? Why would he put it here?

"Send them back to bed," I said. "The kids are just going to be in the way." If it was only adults, I could take more risks.

Alan glared at me. "I decide who goes where." He looked over at Nora, and then the boy. Nora was crying, the boy looked like he was about to hit someone. "Get them out of my sight."

"Go back to bed," Prem said. "I'll be along in a bit to tuck you in."

The boy took Nora's hand and headed back down the hall. So, only us adults. Yes, it gave me more leeway, but still no weapons. Maybe not such a bad thing.

"Where's the money?" I asked. "I guess this was a safe place to keep it until the surveillance?"

Manjeet flicked a glance to the kitchen. In the freezer? No, somewhere out back. No one answered either question.

"Is Kuznetsov leaving town?" If I kept talking, maybe the situation wouldn't escalate. "Is that why you need cash?"

Alan turned his attention from Prem to me. I struggled to keep track of everyone and not just focus on him. Manjeet stepped back toward the kitchen but stopped when he noticed me watching. The only person I couldn't see was Prem, and there was nothing I could do to bring her into my line of sight.

"You don't need to know that," Alan said. "Are you sure you really want me to tell you? Right now, you have nothing on us, and maybe you can live."

I slid my hand in my pocket like I was too calm to worry and shrugged. I didn't have a lot of room in there but enough for my phone, my key ring, and a mini recorder. I bought it when I realized the phone voice recorder app couldn't be turned on secretly. I hit the button to record and said a little prayer to the universe that the thing was charged.

"You're probably going to try to kill me anyway," I said. "It would be nice to know."

Before Alan answered, Prem rushed toward him. "You were going to leave us here? There's a plan, remember. We get out and bring the money to you." She raised her hand to push Alan, but he swatted her away. She stumbled but managed to keep her feet. He pushed her toward the couch.

"Shut up, bitch." Alan pushed her again. This time only to make her sit.

Great. I had all of them in my line of sight, but things were teetering toward out of control again.

"A new plan?" Prem asked. "Why do you need cash? You have millions tucked away in an account somewhere."

Alan cocked his head. I hoped that it was because he heard tires screeching to a halt. But no, he simply laughed. "You should be able to figure it out."

So, not something complicated. I'd pretty much reached my capacity for planning an escape that included me and the children leaving this house alive. Prem was quiet now; physical violence seemed to have been enough to subdue her, or she was thinking about her next step.

Manjeet had snuck a little closer to the kitchen. Maybe going for a gun, but it would need to be well hidden because Child Services would be inspecting on a regular basis. The same for the money. A bag of bills was hard to disguise as something harmless. In fact, maybe the problem was that they'd spent it.

No. You'd need millions to move an organization. No self-respecting gangster would rely on such a weak exit strategy.

"The money is for Alan, not you," I said to Prem. "A few million to set yourself up somewhere out of Kuznetsov's range."

48

"You ou told us it was for the boss, and us," Manjeet said.

Unless he was a very good actor, he was taken by surprise. Alan hadn't denied my allegation, but I needed him to say something totally incriminating otherwise the cops wouldn't be able to hold him. His only hope for living right now sat with the authorities. Kuznetsov would have a contract out on him two seconds after he heard. And he was naive to think there was anywhere in the world he could hide without official help.

"I was right." I took a step toward Alan, so the recorder was likely to get his words clearly. Prem was sulking but I knew better than to write her off. Manjeet focused so tightly on Alan that I don't think he remembered I was there. Another thing I wouldn't take for granted, but I had two goals: to gather incriminating testimony from any one of them, and to keep the kids safe. Getting information on the location of the stash would be a bonus. An even bigger win would be the names of the people inside Child Protection

Services who helped them get away with being a foster family. But that wasn't my current top priority.

"More than a few mil," Alan said. "I've been planning this from the minute I started shifting money around."

"Why here?" I took another step, willing Alan to brag about his plans. "Or is this just the closest stash?"

"I have more, but these two were easy to scare into not stealing."

"We would never be that stupid," Prem said. "You think you are smart? No. We are. We stay on the right side of the boss. No way that money is yours legit."

"He expects people to take a little off the top," Alan said. "I never took so much that he would notice. It's a deep pool."

Enough to give the RCMP the right to interrogate them. Now I wanted him to say Kuznetsov's name. Or even Viktor would be a bonus. I only had minutes until Andy arrived and took over — or made this worse. "Everything I know about mob bosses tells me he knows to the penny what everyone is skimming. And their definition of too much is flexible — is your boss different?"

Prem stood and joined her husband. If they acted together, I was in trouble. No weapons; a blessing and a curse. Two desperate people would always win against one. And I figured Alan wouldn't team up with me any more than I would with him. Whoever they attacked would be on their own, the other would be out the door.

"So where is this stash? More than a few mil is going to be a pretty big package. One you want to grab fast, so not buried in the backyard." I left a little gap in case anyone wanted to blurt out the secret. "Not in the house. Child Services check in too often for that to be safe." Manjeet flicked a gaze through to the kitchen again.

No one had moved while I worked it out. I realized now

that Manjeet and Prem were blocking the path to the back door. I was between Alan and the front door. But I was sure Andy and David would be out there soon. If he wanted to take that escape route, I'd let him.

"The shed seems a bit obvious, and not secure enough." It could be hiding in a shallow basement. Pull up a trap door, grab the package and go. No digging required.

"I'm not telling you anything," Prem said. "Manjeet, go get it. I want them out of here before we're dragged in with him."

So, she was the boss in this house.

"Don't move," Alan said.

"You don't trust him to come back?" Prem asked. "He wouldn't leave me alone. He isn't the kind of guy who would beat his wife, abandon his kid and run away."

Ballsy. What was she trying to achieve?

"If I give the stuff to you, you go, right?" Manjeet said. "It will only take a minute. Like Prem said, I don't run from my family."

One more try to get a name and then I'd encourage Alan to take the offer. Every second that passed could turn into a nightmare or a rescue.

"There's another thing I know about gangsters," I said. "They have their people under surveillance. I guess the life of a major criminal doesn't leave room for trust. The boss must be aware something is going on. How else would Nora end up in this foster home of all the others available?"

Alan glared at me. I hit some target with that comment. "He got her from these two," Alan said. "Viktor and these fucking idiots run the people trafficking. Of course, he'd make sure she came back. Make more on the same asset. Just like Ivan to be greedy."

Bingo.

And then it sunk in. If they sold people for a gang, they weren't stupid. The money wasn't here. Probably given back to Kuznetsov the same day Alan stashed it. And the 'it' Prem meant Manjeet to bring her was a gun. And people traffickers didn't see a kid when they looked at Nora. They saw a payday or a loose end.

Alan still didn't make the connection. He nodded to Manjeet. "Go get it. I'm out of here."

Manjeet stepped into the kitchen, and I moved toward the hall where the kids slept.

"Don't take another step," Prem said. "Empty your pockets."

I considered running, but if Manjeet brought a gun, I wouldn't make it past the front gate. I took out my phone and held it up to show it was off.

"Turn them out."

Fine. If I survived, I would definitely consider everyone a risk in the future, not just the person I was trying to catch. I pulled out the recorder, flicking it off as I did. I regretted not spending the extra for one that would upload my recordings automatically.

Prem reached for the device and tossed it on the floor. Then she stomped on the poor thing until it turned into a scattering of tiny plastic shards.

Manjeet came back and handed his wife a gun.

49

I should never have come inside.

The words kept repeating in my head, blocking out any attempt to change plans. I still needed to get the kids away. I also had to work out a way to gather some kind of damning evidence to replace what Prem destroyed. In addition, I had to avoid getting shot. I suppose I should say try to avoid anyone getting shot, but I didn't feel much sympathy for anyone other than the kids and me.

"No need for that," I said, while I tried to push through the rising panic to a place where I could think. "I'm sure you don't want to leave a mess. It would be better if you disappeared than if you are hunted for murder."

Prem pointed the gun at me, and then back at Alan. I guess the bright side is that they only had one weapon. "We're screwed anyway if the cops come," she said.

I had my phone in my hand, but there was no way I could do anything with it unnoticed. I wished I knew how deep the surveillance went. Did they manage to bug the house? I put my phone back in my pocket just in case Prem decided to do the same as she'd done with my recorder. "They aren't here right now."

"You don't have the authorization to shoot me," Alan said. "I'm protected. If you kill me, Ivan will make sure you regret it."

Why can't he keep his stupid mouth shut? Saying Ivan's name now was no help at all.

"We aren't the ones about to run on him." Manjeet moved from beside Prem to block the front door. "Maybe he doesn't want you shot, but I'm guessing he plans to kill you soon."

"Call him," Alan said. "Find out who he wants dead."

"Let's think a bit," I said. I kept my hands low but turned out, showing I was no threat. "At this moment, it's only us and the kids. The cops will be here soon. I don't think the boss wants to be connected to whatever happens after that."

"Yeah, we don't have much time," Manjeet said. "The brats won't stay under long. We should grab the money and go. Let Alan deal with the boss. We know where to hide. We've done it before."

Interesting. Andy would like that bit of information. I was going to survive this if only so I could pass it on. Giving him a lead was almost as good as clear evidence of Kuznetsov's involvement, but suddenly I wanted the RCMP to take over.

"Probably a good idea," I said. "What did you give the kids? I'll make sure they are fine."

"Not enough to kill them," Prem said. "Maybe I should have done that. Going to sleep permanently is a good death."

Hard to say who was worse. Were all Kuznetsov's people this callous? "They don't need to die," I said.

"They'll talk," Alan said. "Kids always see more than you

think. You should take them with you, or make sure they can't tell anyone about us."

Now it was us again. Alan was either really nuts or smarter than he showed the world. If he could get Prem out of the room, he only had to deal with Manjeet — and me. But those kids would die if his plan worked.

"Children are easy for you to manipulate," I said. "I'm sure they're too traumatized to make sense of what they see. You should take the money and leave us here."

"We should do it," Alan said. "There's plenty for three new lives. Kill her and the kids, and we go."

"Someone will hear the shots," I said. "Just leave us here."

"Shut up!" Prem screamed the words. We'd gotten to her, but not the way I planned.

I glanced toward Alan. His mouth was clamped tight. I turned back to focus on the gun. We were all stuck in place. Manjeet by the front door, Prem blocking access to the back of the house. Me and Alan trapped in the middle. If Alan was my ally, we might have a chance, but this wasn't two against one, it was me against them all.

"Manjeet, call him," Prem said, now calm. "There's no good way out. Let the boss decide."

"What if he says we all die?" Manjeet asked as he pulled a burner from his pocket. "What if he says to wait for him?"

"Then we run, idiot." Prem motioned with the gun for me and Alan to move closer together. We stayed put.

Manjeet left a two-word message and hung up.

I would need that phone when this was over. It would go a long way to replacing my recording. Having the drop number and the code was almost as good as a name. Some technical whiz at the RCMP would find a way to trace it.

"You can't just call him?" Alan asked. "I've got his direct number. Maybe I should make the contact."

"Why?" I asked, still hoping to stop him escalating this to the point that Prem started shooting. "Are you that sure he'll believe your version? What is that, by the way?"

He grinned and seemed to relax completely. "I came by to make sure the merchandise would be ready to sell on. Prem pulled a gun on me. You barged in and made the situation worse."

My stomach turned every time someone made the kids sound like a product. But, as horrible as it sounded, I had other battles to fight first.

"What will you say when he calls, Prem? Assuming he does call. How long will you wait?" I wanted them thinking about anything other than killing everyone and running.

"Exactly what happened," she said. "He'll contact us in a couple of minutes. I'll tell him what Blackhouse tried to do. He'll get us out and deal with the cops, and you."

"Seems like something the boss would delegate," I said.

"Maybe," Manjeet said. "But he'll sort it out. Just keep quiet and wait."

Prem used the gun as a pointer again, motioning Manjeet to pull Alan to me. "Bring the phone here. I'll talk when he calls."

Manjeet dragged Alan to my side. Then stepped toward Prem. Alan shifted his weight to his back foot. He was going for the door.

Not fast enough. Manjeet turned and pushed him to the floor. "Don't fucking make me hurt you." He tossed the phone to Prem. It rang as she caught it.

50

W hat would I give for a couple of seconds where I could turn on my phone?

Apparently, it was going to cost me nothing. Manjeet was busy subduing Alan. Prem looked at the phone. I took mine out and turned it on. I glanced up to see Prem bringing the burner to her face, still looking at the small display screen. No time to open and activate the recording app, but I could hit redial, drop it back in my pocket and hope David would be able to hear the conversation.

Prem turned her attention back to us as she answered the call.

"Yes," she said. I guess the burner didn't have caller ID or she didn't want to risk a name. "That's true."

So, this was going to be one-sided with no names tossed around in an incriminating manner.

Manjeet pulled Alan to his feet and shoved him to the couch. "Don't move."

Alan slumped, like he was giving up. He'd taken his only

shot and failed. I didn't expect it to last, but at least now the room was quiet.

"Where?" Prem asked. "When?"

The person on the other end was issuing orders. Probably about what to do with me and Alan.

"We'll be there." Prem closed the call and tossed the phone into the kitchen. She motioned with the gun for me to join Alan.

I didn't move. The moment I sat down I lost any possibility of escape. I might not be able to make it through the door, but at least I had a chance from here.

"I'm not sitting next to him," I said. "Who called back?"

Prem smirked. "You'll know soon enough. We'll be on our way in a few minutes."

"Where are we going?"

"Let it be a surprise," she said. "Manjeet, get the money."

"I'm not leaving you here alone with them."

She lifted the gun and pointed it at him. "I'll be fine. Get the cash. We need to give it back. You should have listened to me in the first place when I said to tell the boss."

I thought Manjeet was going to argue. His expression tightened with anger. Then he gave a nod and headed through to the kitchen.

"You think giving the money back will satisfy him?" I asked. "Aren't you another couple of loose ends?"

Prem rolled her eyes. It was worse than having the gun in my face. She didn't care about anything.

"Yeah," Alan said. "I'll tell them you knew about the skimming, and you set it up. He'll believe me over you. You sell kids for Christ's sake."

"Yes. We make him a lot of cash on that. Money guys are easy to find. Finding the contacts to buy the product and pass it along, that's a lot of expensive and risky work. He'll be happy we brought you in."

I was pretty sure what would occur if we left this house. First, Alan would take two in the head. Then Manjeet, then Prem, then me. They'd want me to witness the killings, feel the terror of my own death coming.

"What do you think will happen to the kids?" I asked, not caring what she said. It was taking Manjeet a long time to bring the money. I needed to stall enough for me to figure out how to avoid being taken away.

"The boss will get them picked up. He'll deal with them right away. A couple are getting too old to generate the real profit anyway. By lunchtime we'll be relocated and back in business."

I saw Alan fidget on the couch. I needed him to keep quiet so I only had to juggle two high risk actions. If he poked them into violence again, we wouldn't make it out of the house. I glared at him, but he wasn't looking at me to get the message.

"Where is the money?" I asked. "It's taking a long time to retrieve. Maybe Manjeet is on the run?"

"He knows better than to try." Prem glanced into the kitchen as she spoke. "He does what I tell him to do."

"So, you make sure he never learns to get by without you?"

Where the fuck was David? There was nothing to tell me how long we'd been here waiting. In this kind of stress, you can't trust your body. A clock just marks time, no subjective experience to stretch or speed up the seconds.

The back door slammed.

"See. What did I tell you?" Prem said. "Manjeet, bring something to tie them. We need to go now."

Alan jumped up from the couch. "No. I won't go anywhere."

Prem pointed her gun at his foot. "I don't want to shoot, but I will if you make me."

Manjeet tossed two duffel bags on the floor and went back to the kitchen.

Someone banged on the front door. "Police. We're coming in." Andy.

51

"Stay out!" Prem rushed toward me, grabbed my arm, and pulled me close enough to push the gun against my temple. "I'll kill her and the kids if you open that door."

"Gun." I yelled right after, so they knew she was able to follow through.

I had no doubt Prem would pull the trigger and worry about consequences later. The children were safer than me. Prem would need to go down that hall and drag them back to the living room. She couldn't afford the time.

"Manjeet, bring the brats here."

Why do I ever think things will go even a tiny bit my way?

Manjeet didn't answer, just ran down the hall and came back later with a sleeping Nora. He dropped her on the couch and left again, returning with three more, carrying them like they were sacks of meat. When he finished his trips, fifteen kids lay on the furniture and floor. They ranged from a baby to what I guessed was a ten-year-old.

"Mrs. Gupta, let us in," Andy called through the door. "We'll just take the children. They must be in the way, right?"

He was appealing to the nurturing side of a woman who didn't have an ounce of compassion.

She pushed the gun a little harder into my temple.

"Don't try to be the hero. You open your mouth and I shoot you and then Blackhouse and as many of those kids as I have bullets for."

All I could do was watch and remember everything in case we survived. I told myself Andy must have an expert to fall back on for the negotiation. Even if I couldn't see it, Prem must have something to offer to make a deal — or some kind of escape plan. At the first gunshot, the doors would burst, and she'd be lucky to live long enough to regret losing control. I didn't know how much of the reality got through her rage.

"Don't do anything stupid," Alan said. "The boss knows what's going on. He's got people in his pocket who can fix this."

"Manjeet, go check the back door and bring something to shut him up. I need to think."

Again, Manjeet followed orders. He returned with a roll of duct tape and a dish rag. He jammed the rag in Alan's mouth and held it in place by wrapping the tape around his head. It was going to hurt and do some damage when someone eventually removed it. Then he taped Alan's hands and feet.

"They are in the yard," he said while he put the finishing touches on the gag. "Three, with riot gear."

"They won't move unless ordered." Prem released the pressure a little on my head and arm. Not enough for me to make a doomed attempt at escape, or even to say anything, but enough that I didn't need to keep holding my breath to avoid a bullet.

"Her?" Manjeet asked, pointing in my direction with the tape.

"Only her hands and feet." Prem nudged me to put my arms out. "I might need her to do some talking."

He wrapped my wrists a few turns. "Make her sit so I can do her feet."

"No, you get down and do it." Prem pointed the gun at my waist and pushed again. If I survived, I'd have bruises everywhere.

Manjeet looked like he was going to argue this time. I looked at the floor and saw why. There was no room unless he moved two little boys.

"We should use the tunnel," he said, putting the tape on the coffee table and bending to pick up the first boy. "Just gag her and leave them. Take the money and run."

He moved the second boy to a corner across the room.

"How far do you think we can run?" Prem asked. No trace of dismissal in her voice. This time she wanted his answer.

"Far enough," he muttered, still apparently reluctant to get down and restrain me. "We set up somewhere and call the boss."

"What, to kill us?" Prem squeezed my arm tightly. "Forget her feet, go take the bags to the entrance. Let me think."

He shrugged and grabbed the bags to haul them down the same corridor leading to the kids' rooms. A tunnel wouldn't go far in this neighborhood. Too many underground services and no convenient wooded area for a hidden exit.

It had been too quiet outside for too long. Prem was

nervous. If I could get her to loosen her grip, maybe I could use that. But the gun was tight to my side and pointed at a lot of my vital organs.

"What are they doing out there?" Prem asked like I would know. But asking meant she would let me talk.

"Waiting. I mean, I guess they're deciding how to breach without killing anyone. Maybe making sure the neighbors are safely out of range of any stray bullets? Arranging for the power to be shut off?" Certainly not listening in on the whole thing because I called David. I'd somehow forgotten that fact when she put the gun to my head.

"That might work," Prem said. "Even if they cut the power, it won't be too dark."

And the longer they delayed, the less effect it would have. "You should go now."

"And leave you and that asshole to talk?" Prem removed the gun from my side and used it to point at Alan. "You ready to die?"

Not even close. "If you shoot, they'll breach. Why don't you try to talk to them?"

"No. Don't move." She stepped away from me to pull the drapes aside and take a peek. "Fuck."

"What's going on?" Manjeet asked as he came back into the room. "What are we going to do?"

Prem looked back at the room. She took in the whole scene, kids on the floor. Alan gagged on the couch. Nora curled up beside him. Me standing like an idiot. I should have run to the back door as soon as she let me go. But if I did, I'd be leaving those children to take her anger.

"Is the tunnel clear?"

"You want me to go through and check the other end?" It was like he couldn't do anything without her instruction.

"Yes. That's what I meant when I said check out the tunnel."

Manjeet looked at me confused. I wasn't going to help him tell his crazy wife with a gun that she hadn't asked him to do anything other than put the bags at the entrance.

———————

52

"Mrs. Gupta, we're going to call your landline." David this time. "Please pick up so we can work out a solution to this situation."

The phone rang as soon as he finished talking.

"Go check the fucking tunnel," she shouted at Manjeet.

He turned and left. The phone kept ringing.

"You should talk to them," I said.

The cops would hear everything from my phone, and hopefully be recording it, so I reverted back to my original plan. Get them to implicate Kuznetsov with the little added bonus of finding out where the tunnel exited.

"No. They want me to be tied to the phone."

Alan was staring at me like he wanted to say something. It wouldn't be anything useful, so I looked away from him. "The longer you stay here and don't talk, the faster they will decide to breach. Maybe you should head down that tunnel now. It can't be that long, right? Does it go to another house around here?" That would make the most sense. The two of them could sit quietly in another home and wait out the drama.

"How did you know that?" Manjeet asked as he came from the hall.

"You fucking idiot," Prem said. Her language was deteriorating as her panic built. Panic wasn't what I needed. Panic would get her pulling that trigger on impulse.

"No. Just a lucky guess. I would do the same thing. It's probably a good time to go now that the neighbors have been evacuated."

The phone stopped ringing.

Alan started grunting and bouncing on the couch. It worked to get our attention, and he really wanted to say something.

"What?" Manjeet said. "Let me cut off the gag. Maybe he's got an idea."

Prem stepped away from the window, looking around the room like she'd find a solution somewhere in the corner.

Manjeet, apparently tired of waiting for her, pulled out a box cutter and grabbed Alan. He lifted the tape in the middle of the gag, then ran the blade down the center. Alan coughed and sputtered, causing the blade to nick him on the chin. Blood flowed.

"Well," Prem said. "What did you want to tell us?"

The phone rang again. I wished it would stop because I needed to think. And because I was afraid the noise would drown out the voices and no one on the other end of my call would hear anything important.

Alan kept coughing.

"He needs some water," I said.

Someone banged on the front door again. "Mrs. Gupta, you need to talk to us. We would like to make sure the kids are okay."

She raised the gun toward the door.

"No," I said. I wanted to yell but I knew it would have the

opposite effect that I desperately needed. It worked to make her hesitate. "Shoot at a cop and they'll be in here before you can pull the trigger again."

"She's right," Alan choked out. "Just talk to them. Buy some time."

"Time for them to sneak in here somehow?" Prem asked. "I'm not stupid."

"No. You are pretty smart, just stuck." I took a step backward to make it harder for her to shoot us all before someone could stop her. I had to bring her back to a point where she had choices. "You can't shoot us, Prem. If you want to escape, you need to go right now. Take Manjeet and the bags of money and go."

"Mrs. Gupta? Can you confirm that everyone is okay?" David called through the door.

Prem pointed the gun at me. "Tell them you're fine. Don't say who is here, don't say anything about the kids."

"No one is hurt," I shouted toward the door. Obviously, David was putting on an act for the Guptas. He knew exactly what was going on.

"Okay," he said. "Now can we talk?"

"Get away from the door or we'll find out how many times I can pull this trigger before you can stop me."

"Prem, let's just go," Manjeet said. "We'll be fine. We have enough to retire somewhere we can't be found."

"That's what I was going to say," Alan said. "Just go. The boss will take care of you. I'll keep the cops here long enough for you to escape."

"Oh, and then you'll keep your mouth shut?" Prem asked. "You won't tell them anything?"

"Go to the boss. Tell me where the tunnel is so I can go after you get out. I'll wait a few minutes. You'll be safe. I won't follow you after I'm outside."

She was thinking it over. I bit my bottom lip, trying to stop myself from overselling the plan. We would all be safe. Alan wasn't armed. I'd call out as soon as the Guptas disappeared.

"The boss will make you tell him," Manjeet said. Why did he have to grow a backbone now? I much preferred it when he simply followed orders.

"I don't want to know where you are going." Alan shifted so he was perched on the edge of the couch. "Cut me loose. I'll leave and you'll never hear from me again."

"Mrs. Gupta?" David called again. "Please pick up the phone this time."

The ringing started again. Prem's stress level went through the roof. The phone was only inches from my fingers. I didn't care what David or Andy were planning. I needed to stop the noise. I kicked the table, and the headset popped off the cradle. The ringing stopped.

Manjeet ran to pick up the phone.

"Hang up and then take it off the hook." I figured if they had this retro phone, they understood the cops could hear if they didn't end the call.

He looked at Prem who nodded at him. "Do it."

"Will you cut me loose so I can help?" Alan asked. He'd managed to get to his feet. "I can hold the gun on her while you run."

"I'm not giving you a weapon," Prem said. "No one trusts you. For good reason, right? Skimming money from the boss? Stupid."

"Is the boss that powerful?" I asked. "Won't he just cut his losses?"

"He's got too much invested here," Manjeet said. "Too many people on the payroll. No one can touch him."

53

S ay the name! I screamed the words in my head. What I said was, "He doesn't own everyone. And he won't be able to explain away anything that happens when the media arrives."

"I didn't see any TV vans outside," Prem said.

"It won't be long," I said. "Is the boss going to be happy when his business is on the evening news? And all over Twitter?"

Something about that made her stop waving the gun around.

"If you make it any worse, Ivan will come for us," Manjeet said. "Let's just go."

Alan held his hands out. "Cut my hands free. I'll deal with my feet. Just do that and go. Please give me a chance to escape too."

Pathetic didn't work any more than helpful had. This wasn't the first time he'd pissed them off.

The kids were still quiet. I could hear their breathing, so it was probably a good thing, but what had she doped them with?

"Shut up," Prem said. "I need to think."

I had the first name; that would do for Andy. Now we needed this over. The delay had provided Andy plenty of time to find the exit for the tunnel. Or prepare to find them when they left. If they breached now, someone would die for sure. I had to get that gun out of here.

"Maybe just gag him again?" I said. "He's not going to help, you know."

"We can take a hostage when we leave," Manjeet said. "Her? She's living with a cop. They won't risk her life."

Not what I was planning.

"No. Take me," Alan said. "I'm a good hostage. The cops want me for information — I won't give them any — the boss wants me so he can access his money."

Again, not what I planned. If they took Alan, he wouldn't help anyone catch them. But if they wanted to take someone, it would be me or him. The kids couldn't walk on their own, and would only slow them down. And I was pretty sure that as soon as they found a convenient place, the hostage would die.

"You don't need a hostage," I said. "The boss will come looking for you if you take his money guy. The cops won't stop looking for me. Officially or otherwise. Just go."

The threat of Kuznetsov carried a lot of weight. I didn't know if it was enough to make them run alone or take some leverage. Alan was their best bet for using against the boss.

"Why are you waiting?" That was the only thing I couldn't figure out. Not because Kuznetsov would come to rescue them. Not because they wondered what kind of deal they could get for turning over the information they had to the cops. As soon as they decided to take the money, they should have been through the tunnel and gone.

"This was not supposed to happen," Prem said. "We

were going to get out after the next load of kids. He said we would be safe."

So, they'd believed a hardened gang leader when he said they wouldn't be retired with a couple of bullets to the head. Was it the shock of reality keeping them from getting away?

"So maybe he's expecting you to run," I said. "You should do that. When you're free, you can sort it out. Maybe set up somewhere else for him."

Alan laughed. The pathetic act gone. "You can try," he said. "It won't be a bullet, right? No warning. One day, a stranger will bump into you, or you'll drink something you think is safe. Soon you'll feel sick, your hair will fall out and you'll die in a hospital bed because you won't get help in time — no one ever can."

Thank you, Alan, for calming the situation. I swear if I survive, I'm handing everything over to Andy and never doing something this stupid without backup.

"He has to find you first," I said. "He needs to care that you will talk to the cops. It's the only way. Go now."

Prem swung the gun to Alan, then back to me. Then at her husband, and back to Alan. "Shut the fuck up. Manjeet, get the hard drive."

"Good, you have some leverage," I said. "Take it and go. You're running out of time." And so was I.

"You can try," Alan said. "Where would you be safe? Some country without extradition? That's only good for the authorities. Believe me, I've done some research on this."

"I said, shut the fuck up," Prem screamed.

I could see her trembling finger on the trigger now. It wouldn't take much to shoot someone.

Manjeet came back to the room from his last errand. "Let's go." He patted his pocket.

"Fine, run," Alan said. "Maybe you'll be the lucky ones."
Prem lowered the gun and shot him in the thigh.

54

The first cops came through the door before Alan's screams registered in my brain. I yelled at them to be careful of the kids. They hadn't just been dumped. Manjeet had placed them as obstacles to slow everything down.

The back door banged open, and more cops came in yelling at people to get down and drop weapons. Alan hit the floor and started acting the victim. I tried but Prem had me by the arm again and if I dropped, I'd dislocate my shoulder, so I held my hands as far out as possible to show I had no weapons.

Even when you're not the target, the shock and awe approach is terrifying. All I could hope was the cops were in control and not the raging madmen they projected.

Then Andy walked in. He turned to say something to the person behind him, but I couldn't hear the quiet words. Between the gun shot and the yelling, my ears rang, and my brain wanted to go to sleep.

"Put the weapon down now, Mrs. Gupta," Andy said. His voice calm and reasonable.

Prem didn't move.

"It's over," he said.

She squeezed my arm harder.

I kept my eyes on Andy. I really wanted to make sure the kids were okay. To find out where Manjeet had gone to in the seconds between Prem shooting Alan and the door flying open. He might be on the floor just out of my line of sight, or he could have made it to the hall and be free with enough money to start again.

One of the riot gear cops crossed my vision and headed down the hall to where the tunnel started, and the kids' empty bedrooms.

David stepped into the room. I stopped trying to control the situation in my head. It wasn't my job to make Prem drop the weapon. I had to live so David could take me home and tell me I did everything wrong. I had no real argument to make because here I was with a gun to my head.

He stood next to Andy and stared at Prem.

"Where's my daughter?" Alan muttered, even though he was looking right at her. Pretending he was a victim who was concerned about Nora wouldn't get him anywhere.

It wouldn't work. Andy and David had listened to the whole thing through my phone. Everything Alan said about the kids being merchandise. Every detail of his failed escape plan.

"Where's your husband?" Andy asked Prem.

Her hand squeezed my arm. She didn't know either. I tried not to smirk. Manjeet might not be very bright, but he'd been part of this, and having a people trafficker on the streets was a bad outcome.

Then some noise came from down the hall. Dull banging on a wall, a couple of f-bombs ending in a grunt.

The cop who'd gone toward the bedrooms came back

dragging Manjeet by the handcuffs. He tossed him to another officer and stood ready to do what it took to take Prem down.

"Okay, so we're all together now," Andy said. "Put the gun down, let Ms. Deacon go and we can work out a way to resolve this."

Prem didn't let me go. Her anger was clear to me in the tightness of her hold on my arm, and the vibration I felt in her body. Words piled up in my brain, but I kept them inside. Adding more voices to the negotiation would screw everything up. Get me killed, probably the kids, and maybe a cop or two depending on how many bullets she could send our way before someone dropped her.

"Nora?" Alan called.

I had to give him credit for his dedication to the role of distraught parent.

Andy didn't look at him or any of the children. He focused on Prem. His hands held out like mine. He wasn't armed; he didn't need to be. I don't know how many cops stood behind me, but there were three between us and the door, not counting Andy or David. There was no room between them to run even if they didn't shoot as soon as she moved.

"This doesn't have to end badly," Andy said. "You have information we need. Right now, you can negotiate a deal for protection, maybe no prison time. If you fire at anyone else, that deal gets less valuable for you. What do you say? Put the weapon down, come and talk to me."

David was staring at me now and twitching his fingers. Not ASL, a countdown. Five.

To what?

Four.

What am I supposed to do?

Three.

Only one thing I could do.

Two.

I took a breath.

One.

I dropped, letting my body become dead weight and forcing her to let me go or be dragged down with me. I'd deal with the dislocated shoulder if that happened.

I heard yelling again as Prem was pulled back and away.

Then David was there. He wrapped me in his arms and helped me stand. My knees were trembling, and I wouldn't stay up more than a few seconds without him.

"Couch." I had to choke out the word.

He helped me sit and put my head between my knees.

"Deep breaths," he said. "Relax. We've got this." I took a few long slow inhales and exhales. The wooziness retreated enough for me to look up and see the action.

Prem was on her belly, arms cuffed behind her back. A couple of EMTs were checking Alan out and putting pressure on the wound. A scratch. He'd live.

A woman was inspecting the children and talking on a phone. Then more EMTs came through to help the kids.

"Nora? What will happen to her?" I didn't want her disappearing into the system.

"Are you okay now?" David asked. "I'll ask the EMTs to check you before they leave."

"I'm not hurt. What about Nora?"

He kissed my forehead and smoothed my hair. "She's going to the hospital. They'll put her in Glenda's room."

A tear slipped out and he wiped it away. Then another and another. I should be up and asking questions, and I was crying like a girl. I let it happen. Everyone but David was too busy to notice — I hoped.

0

55

The TV vans were pulling up by the time I headed for my car to retrieve all the information I had for Andy. I managed to keep my face turned away. Part of being a successful PI was being anonymous. I'd let the RCMP take all the credit for this one.

The Guptas were on their way to lockup, Alan to the hospital with a couple of armed escorts who would push him into a cell as soon as they treated the flesh wound. The kids were taken to safety with care workers, and Nora on her way to her mother. It was all over except rounding up the leaders of the gang. Of course, they could all be on the lam already.

I headed back to the house with Alan's phone and my notes.

"Can you tell us what happened here?" A woman's voice interrupted my thoughts.

I held my hand to my face to avoid a full capture of my image that could be pasted all over the media. "No comment."

The woman tried to step in my way and pushed her microphone close. "We hear there are children involved."

I kept walking. She had to move so I wouldn't barrel into her shoulder as I passed.

The public doesn't have the right to know my impressions. Andy would give a statement later. All that would make it to the news and the web was my no comments, camera shots of police and RCMP cruisers, and a dark street.

Whichever neighbor called the press, they had no details other than being evacuated.

I ran up the steps and through the front door. Andy and David were in the kitchen at the table. Other cops reporting in. The sounds of a search came from other rooms.

I took the empty seat and waited until Andy was ready for me.

"Okay, what do you have?" Andy said, holding out his hand.

I put the phone on the table and showed him my notes. "I'll send you a copy when I get home, but that book is mine."

"I could just seize it as evidence," he said, flipping through the pages.

"You want me on your side, right?" I pushed the burner toward him. "I need my notes, and I found other information." Not much more than they would have heard.

"Is there anything critical?" Andy asked. "You look like death warmed over. David will take you home. Leave your keys with us; I'll get someone to drop your car off later. You can make a statement tomorrow."

I regretted handing him the notebook. And I didn't want to take David away from this investigation, but I was in no condition to drive. "You heard what happened, right?"

David touched my hand. "We couldn't make out much. Andy recorded it and will try to enhance the sound, but no, we have no idea what was said."

Glad I didn't know that before.

"There's a lot about the boss. I think someone used the name Ivan... yes. Manjeet. Sorry, it's a bit of a mess in my memory."

"Don't worry about it," Andy said. "It'll sort itself out after a rest."

"Two things come to mind. They phoned Ivan or someone with a burner. You might want to trace the calls on it. And did you find the hard drive?"

Andy stopped flipping through my notebook. "What hard drive?"

"It's probably with the money," I said. He looked at me blankly. "You found two bags, right? Just in front of the tunnel?"

"No tunnel, no bags, no hard drive," David said. "Where is this tunnel?"

"But you got Manjeet. He was heading through an escape route. A lot of money in two bags, more than a couple of million according to Alan. The hard drive should be in with the cash because you searched him, right?" Andy called for the constable who caught Manjeet to join us.

"Where did you grab Gupta?" he asked when the guy arrived.

"In the hall. He was coming out of a bedroom, headed back to the hostages."

I pushed myself up from the chair. "Show me. I haven't seen the access, but I can probably guess."

The hall contained four rooms. The first on the right was a bathroom. The second and the one on the left must be the kids' room. All those children crammed into two small bedrooms lined with bunkbeds and mattresses on the floor.

The door at the end was obviously Prem and Manjeet's. It was enormous and had three closets and a nook beside the bed. I closed my eyes and oriented myself. The closet door next to the bed would be the nearest to the outside.

I opened the door, no convenient pile of loot or gaping hole. "Flashlight?" Someone put one of those huge industrial-sized lights in my hand. I tapped on the walls and got the hollow sound on the back wall. I expected a tunnel, not a door to the outside. I leaned back into the room and then looked in the space again. Yeah, the nook on the other side of the bed was deeper than this one.

I found a strap tucked behind a plastic container in the corner. A quick tug and a panel opened up, showing a ladder headed down into the dark.

"You'll find the stuff close to the bottom," I said, handing the flashlight back. "I think this leads to another house." What if they kept more kids in another location?

"Don't worry, we've got it," the constable said. "Thanks, we would never have found it without you."

David pulled me from the closet with a gentle tug. "You did a good job, babe."

"Let's hope it's enough to take Kuznetsov off the street." I was so tired I couldn't find the strength to care. Kuznetsov, the elusive Viktor, no one. I just needed to sleep.

56

I fell asleep in the car on the way home. I remember David tucking me in and saying he was going back to the scene.

I woke up after lunch time, ravenous and with nothing official to do. My notebook was on the night table, so David had come back at least once. And I guess I should be grateful that Andy gave it back.

I showered, dressed and poked through my kitchen for food. Nothing appealing.

Staying inside while the case wrapped up didn't work for me. I grabbed everything, noticing my car keys and a note that it was in the Bayshore lot, then I headed across Georgia Street to the restaurant for a very late breakfast.

There was a text from Andy, requesting my presence at headquarters at four. They were in Surrey, so I'd need to leave an hour at least if I wanted to be on time. Not sure that I did.

I checked my phone for the news while I ate. My 'no comment' had made it to the website, my face was turned away and blurred.

With this case over, I needed to follow up on a few leads for new business, but a day or two off wouldn't kill me.

I left the restaurant and walked over to my car. There was one loose end I could tie up. Glenda and Nora.

Traffic was already building up to rush hour as I made the drive to VGH. I texted Andy to say I'd be late, but no time estimate. Yes, I was screwing with him, but it felt good.

I stepped off the elevator to Glenda's ward and saw her guard, Sean, standing outside her private room. He recognized me and pushed the door open. The curtain was drawn for privacy, so I called out.

"Come through," Glenda said.

She looked healthier. The bruises were colorful, but no machines or IVs flowed from her body. Nora was curled up beside her, asleep.

"How is she?" I asked.

"Fine now," Glenda said. "You almost missed us."

"You got your deal?"

"We'll be leaving for a different hospital in a couple of hours. My stuff is on its way, but they brought my purse and a few clothes for Nora and me."

"Good. Did they tell you what happened?"

Glenda reached for her purse, trying not to wake Nora. The girl stirred and looked at me.

"You saved us," she said.

I smiled and hoped I wouldn't start crying. I usually had more self-control, but the last few days had drained me. "Your mommy missed you."

"We are going on an adventure soon." She wiggled to a sitting position. "Can you come?"

Glenda put her purse on the swing table and pressed the button to raise the bed. "Charity has to stay here. The adventure is just for us."

"Oh." Nora slipped off the bed and went to the side table. "I will draw you a picture so you can remember us." She pulled out a sketch pad and pencils, placed them on the seat of the only chair in the room, sat on the floor and started working.

"She doesn't recall much about last night. The RCMP spared me the details, but I'm sure I'll be told before I go to court. I'm glad you survived." Glenda pulled out her checkbook. "I don't think I'll be able to send you money after I leave, so let me pay now."

"I can get the invoice to you through the proper channels," I said. I felt awkward taking the payment, but I earned it and more.

"No. Go to the bank and cash this or ask for a certified check. I think the account is likely to be frozen soon, but not yet."

"If this is part of the proceeds of crime, I can't accept dirty money." I could accept it, but I wouldn't be allowed to keep it.

"It's clean," she said. "And I've been assured I'll get access eventually. Just don't take the chance that you'll have to wait."

She wrote out the check without asking me for an estimate and handed it to me. Way too much.

"The bill won't be anywhere near the amount."

"I know, but you didn't just do the job. You risked a lot to bring Nora back to me. You saved our lives. I have more stashed away, and I don't need much."

Nora jumped up and ripped the sheet from her sketch book. "You can put it on your fridge like mommy does."

Three people in a park — at least I thought that's what the half page of green meant — drinking tea out of weirdly sized cups. Only us, no Alan. At some point in the future, it was going to come back to her, what awful things she'd experienced, but for now Nora was a happy little girl.

I MADE it to the RCMP headquarters only an hour late. Andy didn't say anything about the time. David was with him in the office, along with some muffins and coffee. I was in favor at least.

"You'll need to testify in court," Andy said without any preamble. "So, make a lot of notes. What you gave us helped. We don't have Kuznetsov yet, but we're closer than before you got involved."

"And the Guptas? Alan?"

"Blackhouse took the deal first," David said. "His first words were 'I have information, I want a deal'. He's going to plead guilty to money laundering. He'll serve time somewhere safe. The Guptas are pleading not guilty, but we've got enough evidence to put them away for a long time."

"And the other children?"

"In good hands," Andy said.

"Any chance you can close down the whole operation?" Ivan probably had replacements already up and running.

"That's the hope," Andy said. "Unfortunately, as long as there's a market, kids will be in danger."

"Is Nora going to stay with her mother?" If they were going to take her away, I needed to know now so I could help prevent it.

"We found no evidence to suggest the adoption wasn't aboveboard. And we're not going to look any deeper," David said. "She'll be safe. I promise."

I believed him. "So, what next?"

David gave Andy a look that I couldn't interpret.

"You are a pain in the ass," Andy said. Then he held up

his hand as I started to argue. "And without you we wouldn't be this far along in the investigation."

"You're welcome." I knew I should stand and leave. I had my money tucked nicely in my account. I had a thank you of sorts. Time to go before something went sideways. Or Michel barged in and spoiled everything.

"Wait," Andy said as I stood. "We use consultants occasionally. I'd like to bring you in on some of our cases."

"Getting Ivan Kuznetsov off the streets?" I was in for that.

"Maybe. I haven't thought that far in advance."

I suspected not everyone was on board with me becoming involved with future investigations. The last time I worked with the authorities, I pissed off a bunch of people, solved the case, and ended up with a boyfriend. "I'll think about it. I have clients and a good relationship with the VPD. I'm not the only pain in the ass in this case."

57

David and I were snuggled up in bed a couple of hours after I left the RCMP office. My body wasn't fully recharged, so we'd decided on dinner in bed.

"What do you think of Andy's offer?" I asked as David topped up my wine glass.

He didn't answer right away, just brushed some pizza crust crumbs off the sheet and into his hand before tossing them into the empty box.

I gave him time. His opinion mattered even though I'd decided to take Andy up on it, at least for a while.

"I like it better when you are simply following up on insurance fraud or cheating spouses."

I laughed. "Those aren't as safe as you seem to think."

"I know. But what Andy wants will put you in harm's way. And not just the kind you get when some guy is going to get mad because he's been caught with a hooker. Organized crime isn't forgiving, and you are an easy target."

"I'm already one." Ivan had seen me. Viktor too probably. The henchmen. Too many people knew who I was. "Won't I be safer working with the RCMP?"

"You're right, but if you back off, you might be okay. Keep going and... I don't want to go to your funeral, Charity."

I sipped my wine while I thought. This conversation wasn't just about consulting on dangerous cases. Yes, Andy was annoying, but he wouldn't put me in danger for the hell of it. To be honest, the only person putting me in danger was me.

"I'm sorry I pushed you away," I said.

"Okay," he said. "Why do you withdraw like that? When you have people around who can help, you run."

"Long history of being told to go home and be a good girl and don't get in the way of the professionals." It was more than that, and this was the time to lay everything out. "And some of my contacts won't talk to me if you're around. And mostly because I don't want to keep fighting about me taking risks."

"I can't promise I won't ask you to be careful," he said, "but I understand. The thing is, when you go solo, I think it's because you are protecting me. That you are going to commit a crime and you want me to be able to deny knowledge of it."

I sat up and stared at him. He was so far from what I thought, I couldn't figure out how he got there. "I don't do it for that reason. I mean, I don't commit crimes you need to ignore."

"Break and enter? Hacking?" He grinned when he said the words, and I started to see the trail of actions leading to his assumption.

"Minor things all PIs do." I flopped back on the bed. "I do turn a blind eye when my contacts are criminals. But nothing the cops would use. I would never give anyone a heads up you were coming so they could get away."

"Does your Hells Angels contact know that?"

"Do I have any secrets?" I didn't feel that gut reaction he was trying to control me.

"Plenty, I'm sure. I don't want to get in your way. I want to help so you are safer when you do reckless things."

"I promise to try," I said.

"And don't let Andy push you around," he said.

"He doesn't have what it takes." I yawned so hard my jaw cracked. David took my glass and tucked the blanket around me.

WANT MORE?

The mob isn't finished with Charity. Use the QR code to join her on her next adventure in WRATH.

~

If you enjoyed reading Pride, please consider helping other readers to find the story by leaving a review.

FREE EBOOK

Claim your copy of Buying Into Death when you use the QR code to sign up for my newsletter and follow Charity as she solves her fastest case yet!

ALSO BY P A WILSON

For more books by P A Wilson

Use the QR code below or go to pawilson.ca

ABOUT THE AUTHOR

Perry Wilson is a Canadian author based in Vancouver, BC who has big ideas and an itch to tell stories. Having spent some time on university, a career, and life in general, she returned to writing in 2008 and hasn't looked back since (well, maybe a little, but only while parallel parking).

She is a member of the Vancouver Writers Social Group, The Royal City Literary Arts Society, and The Surrey Writing Workshop. Perry has self-published several novels. She writes the Madeline Journeys, a fantasy series about a high-powered lawyer who finds herself trapped in a magical world, the Quinn Larson Quests, which follows the adventures of a wizard named Quinn who must contend with volatile fae in the heart of Vancouver, and the Charity Deacon Investigations, a mystery thriller series about a private eye who tends to fall into serious trouble with her cases, and The Riverton Romances, a series based in a small town in Oregon, one of her favorite states. Her stand-alone novels are Breaking the Bonds, Closing the Circle, and The Dragon at The Edge of The Map.

For more information
www.pawilson.ca
pawilson@pawilson.ca

ACKNOWLEDGMENTS

People think that the process of writing is solitary. That's not the case for me. I have help from so many people it would be hard to acknowledge everyone, but I'll give it a try.

The support and inspiration I get from my writer's groups is incalculable. The Vancouver Writers Social Group opens my mind to other ways of telling a story. The Royal City Literary Arts Society gives me the opportunity to meet and share with other writers who have more knowledge than I do. The Other 11 Months group is where I learn about getting the words on the page. And my critique group who helps me find the best parts of the story I want to tell. Thanks to all of the members of these great groups.

Last of all, but definitely a huge part of the process, my beta readers. These are the people who love stories and are willing, and more than able, to tell me if my finished story is ready for you, my readers.

www.ingramcontent.com/pod-product-compliance
Lightning Source LLC
Chambersburg PA
CBHW020315200626
46814CB00006BA/2251